 "Mrs. Allen?" Sam called, as the older woman stepped into her truck. "I don't mean to be rude, but how much is the entry fee for the Super Bowl of Horsemanship?"

"Oh, did I forget to write that in there?" Mrs. Allen tsked her tongue. "Well, my goodness, I guess I'll have to add one more teeny line at the bottom of my flyer." Mrs. Allen watched the girls carefully as she announced, "It will be one hundred dollars per team."

Sam was too surprised to gasp. She heard Jen moan, but neither of them could think of what to say.

Sam and Jen stared after the tangerine-colored truck as it bumped over the bridge, then hit the gravel and fishtailed like a bucking bronc.

"That's a lot of money," Jen said, finally.

"Yes it is," Sam said, but determination was gathering in her.

If she won this race, she'd earn something more important than money. If she won, she'd show Dad she was a good rider, one he didn't need to watch over every minute.

"It's a whole lot," Sam admitted. "But that's not going to stop me."

Read all the books in the PHANTOM STALLION *series:*

Phantom Stallion

❧ 10 ❧
Red Feather Filly

TERRI FARLEY

AVON BOOKS

An Imprint of HarperCollins*Publishers*

Library of Congress Catalog Card Number:
2003092098
ISBN 0-06-056158-0

First Avon edition, 2004

AVON TRADEMARK REG. U.S. PAT. OFF. AND IN OTHER COUNTRIES,
MARCA REGISTRADA, HECHO EN U.S.A.

❖

Visit us on the World Wide Web!
www.harperchildrens.com

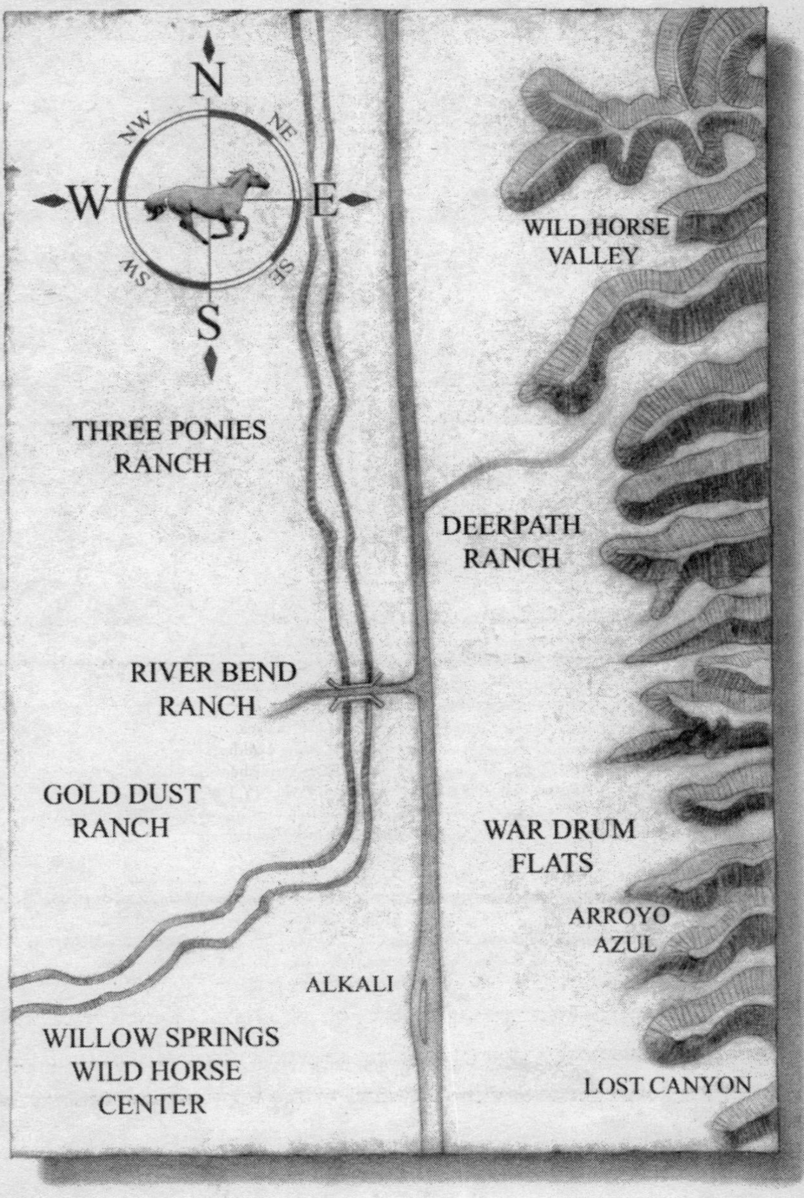
N
NW
NE
W
E
SW
SE
S
WILD HORSE VALLEY
THREE PONIES RANCH
DEERPATH RANCH
RIVER BEND RANCH
GOLD DUST RANCH
WAR DRUM FLATS
ARROYO AZUL
ALKALI
WILLOW SPRINGS WILD HORSE CENTER
LOST CANYON

05801-1601

Chapter One

*O*verhead, two wild geese split off from a ragged vee of birds winging south.

As their flock flew on, the pair turned back, swooping low enough that Samantha Forster heard the silken rush of feathers and saw the glitter of dark eyes studying her.

A dome of blue sky arched over River Bend Ranch. Underfoot, a few shoots of grass ventured through dirt dark from melting snow.

There was a moment of silence from the squadron of construction workers hammering as fast as they could to rebuild the barn while the sunny weather lasted. With permission from Dad, they'd arrived just as the sun was rising. Since six A.M., this was the first time they'd quit pounding.

In the quiet, Sam could hear the La Charla River dashing under the bridge, gurgling over rocks frosted with morning ice.

Northern Nevada was still making up its mind about springtime, but Sam knew it had arrived.

"Samantha, did you hear me?" Dad's stern voice made it clear he knew she hadn't.

"Sorry, what?" Sam felt as if she'd come plummeting back down to earth.

Dad and Brynna sat on their horses, ready to ride out. For a minute, she'd forgotten all about them.

"Honey," Dad said, "that's just what I'm talking about."

What was just what he'd been talking about? Sam tried not to look guilty.

She stared up past Strawberry's roan legs, past Dad's faded jeans, and met his eyes.

"You've got permission to walk the buckskin and to ride Ace. That's it. Don't take it into your head to give Popcorn a try."

"I wasn't—"

Dad held out a hand to keep her from interrupting and Sam wondered how he'd turned into a mind reader. She'd heard Brynna, her new stepmother, talking about getting a rider up on Popcorn pretty soon. Sam wanted to be the first this spring, but she hadn't uttered a word about it to anyone.

"I've seen you eyeing him, Sam. You're not up to it yet." Dad's words stung, even though she knew it was true. "I want to be sure you're clear about this before I go. You're forbidden to mount him unless someone is watching over you. Spring fever can be a dangerous thing."

"I get it," Sam said. For a second, Dad looked like he might mention her tone. Again. But Brynna spoke up.

"She understands, Wyatt," Brynna said.

"Okay," Dad said. He relaxed in the saddle and Strawberry's ears pricked forward, sensing they were about to go. "We're gonna check out the graze in the spring pasture and decide when to move the cattle. We'll probably be a couple hours."

He and Brynna rode out at a trot. Within seconds, their laughter flowed back to Sam. They probably weren't laughing about her, but Dad's criticism still hurt.

You're not up to it yet. She'd only been back on the ranch for about nine months. And she had taken her share of spills. But why did Dad have to rub it in?

She'd find a way to show him she wasn't the worst rider in northern Nevada. But how?

The sudden thunder of nearby hooves made Sam turn back toward the ten-acre pasture.

Nike, red mane streaming as he paced along the fence, had spotted the halter in her hand. He stopped and tossed his head, attracting the attention of other horses. Tank, the big bald-faced bay, joined Nike. Soon Amigo and Buff jostled each other in excitement.

Behind her, Ace and Sweetheart created a commotion inside the round pen. The high-sided corral had been their home since an earthquake destroyed the old portion of the barn and their attached corrals.

The horses had adapted to the pen, but they missed the open view they'd had of the ranch. Now they spent their days peeking between the fence rails.

The two horses had snorted a greeting when Sam had passed by on her way to the damaged tack room to get Dark Sunshine's halter. They'd been patient when she'd walked by without stopping for them. But now that it looked like she might be leaving with another horse, they neighed in protest.

"It's okay, boy," she called to Ace, letting him know he wasn't forgotten.

The long minutes Ace had been trapped in the fallen barn had reminded Sam how much she loved her little bay mustang.

"Jen will be here soon and then I'll get you out of there."

In the bad weather, most ranch work had been done from a pickup truck instead of on horseback. These were working horses and their vacation had left them full of energy.

In the pasture, Buff lifted his furry brown body into a half rear. The others shifted to give him space, but their ears remained pricked forward and their eyes watched Sam.

"You'd think I had a bucket of oats instead of a halter," Sam told Blaze.

The Border collie pranced beside her, tail waving, mouth open, as he escorted her to the pasture.

Popcorn finished rolling in the mud, heaved himself to his feet, and shook. His white coat was wet and smeared with brown. He'd noticed he was missing something and trotted to join the others by the fence.

Only one horse hung back.

Dark Sunshine ignored the saddle horses' excitement and stared toward the Calico Mountains. She turned one ear to catch Sam's boot steps, but her head stayed high, her attention focused.

"The only horse on the place who isn't fascinated," Sam told Blaze, "is the one I need to catch."

Blaze panted sympathetically.

"Get back," Sam ordered the other horses, but they didn't.

She jiggled the latch on the gate, then waved her hand.

Filled with high spirits, the crowding horses rolled their eyes and backed away. They'd had breakfast two hours before, but they were still checking to see if she carried food. She wasn't, so they worked off their energy with a gallop around the pasture.

"Blaze, you stay," Sam said as the dog tried to follow her.

The dog's fanning tail drooped as Sam let herself into the pasture and latched the gate. She took advantage of the horses' distraction to stride across the wet earth and new grass of the pasture. It was only sensible to get over to Dark Sunshine before the saddle horses grew bored and returned to her. Excited and heavy, they could bump the pregnant mare off her feet without meaning to and a misplaced hoof could cause an injury.

"And we don't want that," Sam said out loud. "We only have about eight weeks left."

She'd kept talking as she walked. She meant her voice to ready the mare for her approach, but she might as well have stayed silent.

In her eight months on River Bend Ranch, Dark Sunshine had grown accustomed to life as a captive mustang. She took comfort in her adopted herd, but she didn't trust humans. She tolerated Sam's presence.

"But you don't like me, do you, girl?" Sam asked.

The mare raised her head higher. Her black-edged ears pointed east. Her dark-gold skin shivered in annoyance. Sam didn't blame the mustang for hating captivity, but the graceful, deerlike mare's belly was rounded in pregnancy. And that changed everything.

Dark Sunshine's eyes stared toward the mountains as if she ached to be there.

"Do you miss him, or your freedom?" Sam asked.

The mare was in foal to the wild silver stallion known as the Phantom. That was a great gift and a burden. With two wild parents, the foal could be born rowdy and uncontrollable.

Dad hadn't said Sam could keep the foal for her own, but he hadn't said she couldn't.

"C'mon girl," she said. "We have the ranch to ourselves."

Dad had given the cowboys the day to go to a saddle show in Reno.

Gram had driven into Darton to do the month's grocery shopping. As she'd made her list, Gram had muttered about making lasagna and mentioned to Sam that it had been her mother's favorite dinner, one she'd elbowed Gram out of the kitchen to make.

Gram had smiled at the memory, but she must have sensed Sam's melancholy as she thought of her long-dead mother.

"You're thirteen years old, for heaven's sake," Gram had scolded. "It's past time you learned to cook and I say you should start with lasagna, this weekend."

But that would come later.

Dark Sunshine started at the sound of a vehicle turning off the highway. Tires grated on the patch of gravel road just before the bridge.

Sam couldn't see much from here, but it didn't sound like one of the ranch trucks. Still, it sounded vaguely familiar.

Then, hooves clopped on the bridge.

Sunny shied and jerked as if Sam had reached for her. When Sam started to back away, the mare bolted in the opposite direction. She stopped to watch, though, as Jen arrived on a galloping palomino.

Silk Stockings burst into the ranch yard in a

flailing lope, demonstrating why she'd been nick-named Silly.

Jen's turquoise sweater outlined arms braced to keep her horse's head up. She appeared to be using all the strength in her seat and legs to drive the mare forward so she wouldn't buck.

When she was almost upon Sam, the palomino began shaking her head. Her white mane and fore-lock flipped around her, and the mare wore a shame-faced expression. But Jen didn't punish her horse.

"My fault," Jen called as she slowed the palomino to a jouncing trot, then a walk. "I thought two sec-onds about sharing the bridge with Mrs. Allen's truck, then two more seconds about what a crazy driver she is, and that was all it took. Silly read my mind and took off."

Jen rode past, hands and voice comforting Silly. Sam envied Jen's controlled understanding of her mount. Many riders would have jerked at the reins, forgetting the punishment the bit inflicted on a tender mouth. Others would have yelled and blamed the horse for their own miscalculations.

Not Jen. As she turned Silly to come back at a smooth, long-reaching walk, the palomino looked proud and collected.

"One of the best things about Silly," Jen said, dis-mounting, "is her short attention span. She's already forgotten we were scared, haven't you girl?"

Sam laughed as Jen patted the palomino's neck

and let her go to the end of her reins. With high-flung head and tail, Silly greeted the other horses.

"Wait," Sam said as Jen's words soaked in. "Did you say Mrs. Allen?"

As she asked, a tangerine-colored truck rocketed across the bridge and into the River Bend Ranch yard.

"Oh, yeah," Jen said. She lunged and grabbed Silly's reins just under her chin.

Blaze began barking. Red hens fled cackling for the safety of their coop.

With a squeal of brakes, a jerk, and a sputter, the pickup's engine died.

Sam stood close to Jen.

What could be so urgent that Mrs. Allen had arrived in a cloud of dust on a Saturday morning?

Chapter Two

"Do you know what would happen to us if we drove like that?" Sam gasped.

"We'd be grounded for life," Jen said, in a level tone. "And we'll remind each other of that when we finally get driver's licenses, right?"

"Right. I like Mrs. Allen, but she drives like—"

"A grasshopper in a chicken coop," Jen finished. "That's what my dad says."

Remembering one morning when she'd been late to school and Mrs. Allen had driven her, Sam decided Jen's father was right.

Now, Mrs. Allen scooted out of her truck. She slammed the door in time to confine two little black-and-white dogs. Yapping and jumping, they ricocheted like jumping beans off the walls of the truck cab.

Dad had told her the dogs were a breed called Boston bulls and they were naturally high-strung. Still, Sam wondered if the dogs had been that way *before* they started riding with Mrs. Allen.

"Imp, Angel, behave," Mrs. Allen ordered, then shook her head.

Mrs. Trudy Allen lived across the river, on the edge of mustang country, at Deerpath Ranch. Just months ago, she'd taken in thirteen "unadoptable" wild horses and christened her project the Blind Faith Mustang Sanctuary.

Until then, most people across the county said she was eccentric. Sam knew they meant *crazy*, but because Mrs. Allen was an artist, they'd found a nicer way to say it.

Today, Mrs. Allen didn't look crazy. She carried a leather folder. Her hair, dyed inky black, was pulled back in a low ponytail to show round copper earrings. She wore a black-and-copper knit sweater with boots and a black skirt. Or maybe it wasn't a skirt. As she walked toward the girls, Sam tried to figure out exactly what Mrs. Allen was wearing.

"Are those gaucho pants?" Jen asked.

"Fashion is not my thing," Sam said. "But she looks pretty dressed up—"

"And arty—"

"—for a Saturday morning," Sam finished.

And for her age, she added silently. Despite her

fashionable outfit and lively brown eyes, Mrs. Allen was about seventy years old. But she didn't walk with the vague wandering gait she had a couple of months ago. Since she'd adopted the horses, she moved like someone much younger.

"Morning, ladies," Mrs. Allen called. "Jennifer, that was a fancy piece of riding you pulled, cutting in front of my truck and galloping for the bridge."

"I . . ." Jen began.

"And Samantha, I take it you're alone here?"

"I . . ." Sam echoed.

Mrs. Allen brushed aside their comments. "The thing is, I've been trying to call Grace for over an hour."

"Gram's in Darton," Sam explained.

"Figured something like that. I was driving into Darton myself when I saw Jennifer headed this way, though, and got to thinking. You're in Journalism class, right?"

Sam nodded.

"And you"—Mrs. Allen turned toward Jen—"you're smarter than you need to be for most all normal purposes."

"Smart enough for what?" Jen asked. Her tone indicated she wasn't taking any chances.

"To help me out," Mrs. Allen said.

Sam waited without saying a word. She liked Mrs. Allen a lot, especially for her mercy toward the wild horses. But she'd spent a miserable, hand-blistering week helping to repair Mrs. Allen's broken-down fences and she knew the old woman didn't mind getting someone to do work for free.

"What I'd like is for you to read something for me," Mrs. Allen said, gesturing with the leather folder. "Tell me if it says what I want it to say."

How hard could that be? Sam looked at the slim folder and decided it wouldn't take long.

"Why don't you tie Silly and we'll go into the house," Sam offered. She didn't want to, really. She'd rather be saddling Ace and riding out with Jen, but she'd been raised to be a good neighbor.

"I'd appreciate the help," Mrs. Allen said. "And I wouldn't turn down a cup of coffee and some of Grace's baking."

Mrs. Allen and Gram had been friends for years. While Mrs. Allen became a painter, Gram learned the art of running a ranch, and everyone knew that Gram's pies, cakes, and cookies were the best. Who could blame Mrs. Allen for inviting herself in for a snack?

"I don't know about coffee," Sam said, "but Gram made butter cookies last night. We couldn't have eaten all of them."

Mrs. Allen's divided skirt billowed around her as she stepped out ahead of the girls and walked toward the house.

Jen paused to wind Silly's reins over the hitching rail and the screen door slammed as Mrs. Allen went into the house.

Sam gave a helpless shrug and met Jen's eyes. "I want to go ride," she mouthed silently.

Jen nodded so hard, her flaxen braids flapped and her dark-rimmed glasses slipped partway down her nose.

Indoors, Mrs. Allen had already poured herself a cup of coffee. She took a sip, then blinked.

"This is some strong, crack-of-dawn coffee," Mrs. Allen said, stifling a cough.

Jen twirled one braid impatiently, and Mrs. Allen laughed.

"You two love horses, don't you?"

"Yes."

"Of course," Sam said, her voice overlapping Jen's.

"And how do you feel about money?"

"Good if it's mine, and embarrassingly jealous if it's not," Jen said, but a note of interest sharpened her voice.

"By the time you've taken a look at this"—with a broad smile, Mrs. Allen tapped the leather folder positioned on the kitchen table—"you'll thank your lucky stars you got a head start over all the other riders in northern Nevada."

Sam rubbed her hands together in anticipation. Jen dashed her bangs back from her glasses, as if seeing better would help.

Chuckling over the girls' excitement, Mrs. Allen dipped her hand toward the kitchen table.

"How about we pull up some chairs and have a little conversation?" Mrs. Allen settled herself.

As soon as the girls had done the same, she withdrew a sheet from the leather folder and handed it to Jen.

"The Super Bowl of Horsemanship?" Jen read from a typed page.

"Yes, indeed," Mrs. Allen said proudly. "Right here in your own backyard."

"I don't think I've ever heard of it," Sam ventured. She didn't want to sound ignorant about something to do with horses, but she really hadn't.

"That's because I just created it," Mrs. Allen said. "And first prize is enough money to make your head spin."

That wouldn't take much, Sam thought. She'd love to buy a new saddle. The one she used looked just like what it was—a handed-down kid's saddle. She'd been looking at tack catalogs, dreaming about a new one. Even though she'd earned some money of her own, Dad wouldn't let her touch it until she was ready for college.

Sam scooted her chair closer so that she could read the typed page right-side-up.

"You created it. And you're giving away a percentage of all the entry fees collected," Jen read carefully. Then, she turned her head so that the kitchen light glinted on her glasses, making her look owlish. "*What* percentage?"

When Mrs. Allen busied herself with another cookie instead of answering, Jen focused on the typed sheet once more. "Let's just see what we have to do to win."

Sam knew that blurry tone of Jen's. It was the same one her voice took on when she was studying.

Mrs. Allen leaned back and savored a butter cookie while Sam and Jen read silently.

The Super Bowl of Horsemanship required horse and rider to complete an "extreme" obstacle course like those used for training police horses. It would include loud noises, visual distractions, and surprises to test the horse's confidence in his rider. After a short quarter mile of chaos, the race would cover seven miles of rough terrain.

Sam smiled as she studied the course map. She could already see herself winning. She knew every foot of sagebrush and alkali flat that made up the course.

Leaving from Deerpath Ranch, the race headed straight across the range for La Charla River. Once through the river, the trail turned south. It passed right by River Bend, then turned east at the Gold Dust Ranch. There, the racecourse crossed the river again, before running across War Drum Flats and back to the finish line at Deerpath Ranch.

A thrill of excitement tickled up Sam's arms and legs. She wasn't the best rider around, but she and Jen rode that territory all the time. Familiarity had to count for something, didn't it?

So, why wasn't Jen hooting with joy?

Sam stared at the map, wondering what she'd missed.

"What are these?" Sam asked, tapping a symbol on the map.

"Vet check points," Mrs. Allen explained. "Dr. Scott—you know, that nice young veterinarian— helped plan the course. This is not an endurance race, because you wouldn't have time to train for it."

When Mrs. Allen pointed out the date printed on the sheet, Sam looked. It was only two weeks away, on the last weekend of spring break.

"Even though the race isn't too demanding, Dr. Scott thought vets should check each horse twice." Mrs. Allen held up two fingers. "Before the race and at the finish line. If the animals show the slightest sign of abuse, the riders will be disqualified."

Sam nodded. "Good deal," she said. "That'll keep people like you-know-who from winning the race, but ruining a horse."

"You needn't spare Linc Slocum's feelings on my account," Mrs. Allen said with a sniff. "He doesn't know a thing about keeping his horses safe and healthy."

"That's because he still hasn't figured out that they aren't cars," Jen grumbled. "If my dad weren't his foreman, I don't know what would happen to Linc's horses."

"I'll tell you," Mrs. Allen said. "If that big beautiful Champ he rides should ever decide to run away from home, he can come to my house."

They all nodded and reached for more cookies, as if sealing a pact.

"Wait," Jen said, as her eyes returned to the rules. "Number three is a weird rule."

"It's my favorite," Mrs. Allen said.

Sam read rule three aloud. "'Competitor must be part of a co-ed team . . .'?"

"A male and a female," Mrs. Allen clarified, as if Sam weren't very bright.

"I know what it means!" she said, exasperated. "But—"

"Keep reading, Sam," Jen said as she skimmed ahead.

"'Together, each team rides the course side by side'!"

"The entire course?" Jen asked. "You couldn't divide it up so that each rider had, say, 3.4 miles—"

"No, Jennifer. Side by side. But you don't have to hold hands."

"Good thing," Jen said. "If you were riding with someone stubborn as a rock, like Jake Ely, and you fell while you were winning . . ." Jen rolled her eyes.

"You might get your arm dislocated from your shoulder socket," Sam said.

"Are you kidding?" Jen asked. "He'd just keep galloping and expect you to keep up!"

Although she laughed, Sam pictured herself galloping beside Jake. They would absolutely win, if he
rode Witch and she rode the Phantom. She could see
it as if it were a movie. Black legs would stretch to
keep up with white. Milky tail would stream just
ahead of midnight-black tail as they sped across the
range, leaving all the other riders so far behind, their
shouts of dismay would fade into silence.

But the whole idea was impossible. No one could
know, *ever*, that she'd ridden the Phantom.

"That particular rule is what will keep my race
from becoming a free-for-all," Mrs. Allen said. "A
man and woman, or"—she paused and smiled meaningfully—"girl and boy, will have to travel at the
speed of the weaker partner. The two who are most
evenly matched will win."

"It's a great idea," Sam admitted, as her hopes
deflated.

There was no way she and Jake would ride
together. Even without the Phantom.

Jake's riding ability was ten times better than
hers. And Jake, as the youngest of six brothers,
longed for a truck all his own. The prize money
would put him lots closer to buying one, so he couldn't
make a decision based on friendship. He'd be foolish
to take her as his partner.

He'd be better off riding with Jen. Of course they
didn't get along, but that wouldn't matter. Jen and
Jake were both stubborn and determined. If the

reward was something they both wanted, they'd work toward the goal together.

Sam sighed. Of course she could still enter. There were other boys she could ride with, right?

Her logical mind just couldn't come up with anyone. Ryan Slocum, the polished horseman from England, deserved a better partner. Pepper, who could spin a loop with his lariat and actually ride Nike through it, had to know a real cowgirl who could keep up with him. Of course, there was always Dad. Or was there? With a chance at all that prize money, he'd probably want Brynna by his side.

Sam crossed her arms and stared at the piece of paper as if the name she sought would bob to the surface in bold print.

Apparently Jen hadn't veered off on the partner tangent the way Sam had, because she was still studying the sheet.

"And it's a benefit for the sanctuary," Jen read.

"To tell you the truth, girls, I made a serious error, starting the sanctuary in such a hurry. Oh, not in adopting those horses," she said, smiling. "But I wasn't very organized about it. I pretty much let my heart rule my head, and now I'm trying to catch up. You know the indoor arena I was building?"

"Oh, yeah, that's going to be so cool. You can . . ." Sam faltered. "*Was?*"

"I heard that you lost it in the earthquake," Jen said sympathetically. "Clara at the diner told my dad," she added to Sam. "Five point one on the Richter scale is no little jiggle. It could have smashed everything around here into toothpicks."

"Thanks for the scientific analysis, dear," Mrs. Allen said.

She didn't sound sarcastic, so Sam had to ask the question she'd been asking neighbors since the earthquake. "Mrs. Allen, did your dogs know the earthquake was coming?"

Every horse on River Bend had acted strange before the earthquake. Popcorn, Ace, and Sweetheart had been the most unsettled, except for Tinkerbell, the sweet, draft-cross mustang Sam had been lucky enough to rescue from a slaughterhouse.

"No, they didn't," Mrs. Allen answered. "I heard most everyone's animals acted odd the week before." Mrs. Allen frowned. "I even asked Dr. Scott about it, and do you know what that young man had the nerve to say?"

Sam and Jen both shook their heads.

"He said that driving around with me had . . . oh, how did he put it? It was not complimentary." Mrs. Allen's index finger tapped her temple. "Oh, yes. He said riding with me had 'knocked their early warning systems out of whack'!"

Sam couldn't help giggling, even when Mrs. Allen gave her a quelling look.

"But the point is," Mrs. Allen raised her voice, "the arena wasn't insured."

Sam bit her lower lip. A month ago, she would have ignored this talk of insurance. It had been no big deal, simply something adults complained about, until the earthquake. Now, she understood. Gram and Dad had congratulated each other and thanked heaven they'd kept up the insurance payments on River Bend, even during the hard times. Because now, the insurance company was paying to rebuild the barn.

Sam watched as Mrs. Allen pretended to be very busy brushing cookie crumbs from her sweater.

Everyone thought old Mrs. Allen was rich, but was she? Sam's mind circled back to the question Mrs. Allen had ignored before.

"Will the prize money be very much?" Sam blurted.

"Very smooth, Sam," Jen said, grimacing.

Sam felt a hot blush cover her face.

"I need enough to keep construction going until my next check from the gallery in New York," Mrs. Allen explained, not looking nearly as embarrassed as Sam felt.

Mrs. Allen still hadn't spelled out how much prize money they'd be racing for, but Sam gave up. It would be rude to keep pressing her.

In the moment of uneasy silence, Sam's kitten, Cougar, now a leggy "adolescent," padded into the kitchen.

"Mew?" he asked, walking away from his water bowl to sniff Blaze's empty dog food dish before vaulting into Sam's lap and making himself comfortable.

Mrs. Allen slid the typed sheet across the table, then put it back inside the leather folder. "You think it's all right, then? Good enough to have flyers made?"

"I think everyone in the county will want to do it," Jen said. "I'm already wondering who I'll get to ride with me."

"Me too," Sam admitted, and for an instant her eyes met Jen's.

She looked away. She hated the feeling that flashed between them.

She and Jen were best friends, not competitors. They couldn't be. Jen was a much better rider. She didn't fear going too fast, or jumping or falling. Once Jen mounted a horse, she belonged there.

The Super Bowl of Horsemanship. Sam imagined a booming voice reading tall golden letters. If she rode in it, no one would think she was afraid. If she won, everyone would forget her accident. She might forget, too.

"I'll post the flyers at Clara's Diner and the general store there in Alkali," Mrs. Allen began.

"What about Crane Crossing Mall?" Sam said. "There's a bulletin board at the Western wear store—"

"Tully's," Jen put in.

Mrs. Allen nodded, stood, and swooped the folder up from the table.

"I'll drop a copy at the *Darton Review Journal*," she said, walking toward the door. "Who knows? They might want to do a newspaper story on it."

The girls followed her outside, but they stopped when they saw a black horse tethered next to Silly.

It was Witch, but Jake was nowhere in sight.

"Hey, Witchy," Sam said.

The black mare flattened her ears and glared in a way that indicated she didn't appreciate the nickname.

She'll eat you alive, Jake had warned her once, so Sam kept her hands to herself and stared at Witch's bridle.

Witch wore a mushroom-brown split-ear headstall. Faint feathers were etched on the leather. Sam recognized it at once. She'd given it to Jake on his sixteenth birthday, months ago, and paid for it with her own money. That was the last time Dad had allowed her to spend more than a few dollars.

That fact and the sudden creak of Mrs. Allen's truck door made Sam think of something.

"Mrs. Allen?" she called after her. "I don't mean to be rude, but how much is the entry fee?"

"Uh-oh," Jen said. She began shaking her head, amazed she'd forgotten to ask such an obvious question.

"Oh, did I forget to write that in there?" Mrs. Allen tsked her tongue. "Well, my goodness, I guess I'll have to add one more teeny line at the bottom of my flyer." Mrs. Allen watched the girls carefully as she announced, "It will be one hundred dollars per team."

Sam was too surprised to gasp. She heard Jen moan, but neither of them could think of what to say.

Sam and Jen stared after the tangerine-colored truck as it bumped over the bridge, then hit the gravel and fishtailed like a bucking bronc.

"That's a lot of money," Jen said, finally.

"Yes, it is," Sam said, but determination was gathering in her.

If she won this race, she'd earn something more important than money. Sam braced both hands against the hitching rail. She gripped it so hard, her nails bit into the wood. If she won, she'd show Dad she was a good rider, one he didn't need to watch over every minute.

"It's a whole lot," Sam admitted. "But that's not going to stop me."

Chapter Three

As the crunch of Mrs. Allen's tires faded, Jen shrugged.

"I don't know why I'm even thinking about that race. It's pretty unlikely a hundred-dollar bill will just flutter out of the sky and into my hand."

"I bet your partner could pay," Sam hinted as her eyes locked onto Jen's and held them.

"You're crazy," Jen said. She threw one white-blond braid over her shoulder, turned away from Sam, and paid a lot of attention to making sure the stirrup on her saddle was centered on the leather.

"You know who I'm talking about," Sam said.

"I haven't the faintest idea what kind of warped ideas are in your twisted mind," Jen said, smoothing her fingers between Silly's cinch and her palomino belly. "And I don't want to know."

"Ryan Slocum," Sam said before Jen could cover her ears.

To give her friend time to cool down, Sam strode toward the round corral to catch Ace.

"Remind me why I started hanging around with you," Jen shouted after her. "Because I sure can't remember."

"Yeah, yeah," Sam called back.

Jen had had a crush on Rachel Slocum's twin from the first time he'd knocked on her door to say a mountain lion was eating a nearby buffet. Jen said the way Ryan's sleek coffee-colored hair got messy as he rode made her want to brush it off his forehead. Sam didn't understand *that* at all.

She agreed that Ryan's British accent was sort of cool, but it didn't give her the goose bumps Jen reported.

Could that be because Ryan was a Slocum? Sam tried not to be judgmental. It wasn't Ryan's fault he'd been born into that family. And he had proven himself more trustworthy than his father Linc and twin Rachel. But he'd also kept Golden Rose, a horse that didn't belong to him, captive in a nearby ghost town instead of reporting her to the sheriff.

Jen knew that as well as Sam did—after all, Golden Rose belonged to the Kenworthys—but she apparently didn't think about it much.

Sam led Ace back to the hitching rail and tied him by his halter rope. While Ace and Silly snorted and touched noses, expressing pleasure at seeing each other, Sam watched Jen.

"Well? Am I right?" she asked, finally. "Wouldn't he be the perfect partner for you?"

"I wish," Jen said, sighing.

"It's only obvious you guys should ride together," Sam said matter-of-factly. She gave Ace a quick brushing, then threw on his saddle blanket.

"Right," Jen said. "But he could pick someone better."

"Like who?" Sam asked. She lifted her saddle into place, knowing her words weren't flattery. She couldn't think of a better girl rider than Jen.

"Like you," Jen suggested.

"Oh, yeah," Sam said. She tried to laugh, but couldn't. "I fall off and get trampled about once a month. I'm sure that's just what any guy looks for in a riding partner. Someone he'll have to spend extra minutes on, peeling up off the desert floor."

Eyes closed, Jen shook her head, blocking out Sam's words.

"You're a good enough rider to do this," Jen persisted.

"Good enough to finish, maybe, but not to win." Sam took a breath, then she confessed, "My dad thinks I'm hopeless."

"That's ridiculous," Jen said before Sam could tell her about that morning. "He thinks you're a fine rider, but he's paranoid like every other father."

"More than most fathers," Sam insisted.

"I'm the one whose parents wouldn't let her go to *school* because of bad influences, so don't tell me about protective." She sighed and looked serious. "You know he's afraid you'll get hurt like you did before."

Sam finished saddling Ace in silence. Jen hadn't changed her mind about Dad, but she didn't feel like arguing.

"Wait, we were talking about you riding with Ryan. How did we get off on this tangent about me?"

"Because it's your kind of race," Jen said. "You connect with your horse. If I understand what Mrs. Allen has in mind, that's what half this race is about."

"Maybe," Sam said, shrugging.

But Jen was right. She might not be dynamite in the saddle, but she could usually communicate with horses.

Ace's head swung around to face her. His black forelock parted over the white star on his forehead and his big brown eyes studied her.

Sam leaned forward and kissed his nose before bridling him. Maybe it was Ace, not her, who was psychic. Of course, she had stayed in touch with the Phantom.

Sam stared past the ranch gates, toward the Calico Mountains. It was spring. He should be nearby. If she could beckon him to the river tonight, she'd do it.

Ace's back hooves danced, eager to be off. Witch flattened her ears and lashed her tail in annoyance.

"Where's Jake, do you think?"

"He's out there, working on the bunkhouse, see?" Jen nodded toward the half-finished structure.

Of course he was. She'd heard all the racket and dismissed it as the carpenters pounding on the barn.

But Jake wasn't hammering. Using a handsaw, he was cutting lumber. His black hair had worked loose from its rawhide tie. Now, it swung forward with each stroke of the saw. As they watched, he dropped the saw, shrugged off his plaid flannel shirt, and tossed it toward a stump. It missed and hit the ground, but he kept working, oblivious to the fact that he only wore a plain white tee shirt over jeans.

The sight of Jake's bare arms made Sam shiver. The sun was out, but it was not warm.

If Dad had asked him to come over and work, why hadn't he mentioned it?

Sam knew Dad hadn't. The insurance company was paying the carpenters repairing the barn. They would move on to the bunkhouse as soon as they'd finished. Dad wouldn't ask Jake to work without paying him. And Dad couldn't afford to pay Jake when he already had a crew drawing wages from the insurance company.

Besides that, Jake was on the school track team. Once the season had started, he used every spare minute to train for his long-distance events.

Jake's saw rasped through the lumber, and sawdust flew. He could have used Dad's electric saw, but he seemed to welcome the exertion.

He didn't look over at her and Jen even once.

Was he just concentrating or was he angry?

Sam took Ace's bridle reins and backed him away from Silly and Witch.

"I don't think I want to talk with him," she said to Jen.

Sam stepped into her stirrup, swung into the saddle, and turned Ace toward the ranch entrance.

"He's sawing like he's taking someone's head off," Jen said as she mounted, too. "So, I'm sure not going over there."

"How 'bout later?" Sam asked.

"Okay," Jen said. "We'll take care of everything after our ride, for sure."

But after their ride, Jen chickened out.

"It's getting too cold to work with the horses," she said. "And Jake hates me even when he's in a good mood."

"He doesn't hate you," Sam said, but Jen had a point. She and Jake were too much alike to get along.

So, Sam waved as Jen turned south, leaving her to ride back to River Bend Ranch alone.

Gram would be there when she arrived, though. She and Jen had seen the big yellow Buick go by on the highway.

"I saw Gram's shopping list before she left," Sam told Ace as she rubbed his damp neck. "And if you're very good, I'll bring you a sugar cube for a treat. She doesn't mind spoiling you."

Ace lifted his head a little higher. The little

mustang's vocabulary couldn't include the word "sugar," but he sure seemed to understand.

Even before she'd finished crossing the bridge, Sam spotted Gram.

Dressed in a denim skirt and a pale blue blouse with flowers embroidered across the yoke, Gram hefted a sack full of groceries from the Buick's trunk.

Sam rode into the ranch yard, calling to Gram, "I'll be right back and help you."

Ace veered toward the water trough. Sam let him go, but drew rein and dismounted before he could drink.

"Don't allow that horse more than a few mouthfuls, now," Gram cautioned.

"Okay," Sam said.

It was a good thing Gram was too far away to hear Sam's irritated sigh. She hadn't overwatered a hot horse since she was a child. She was pretty sure she hadn't done it then.

"Enough, good boy," Sam said, then walked Ace around for a few minutes before taking him to the hitching rail, slipping his bit and loosening his cinch.

"I got everything we'll need for lasagna," Gram said, as she and Sam filled their arms with sacks. "Pasta, cheese, Italian sausage, and all kinds of good things."

Once they'd juggled their loads into the kitchen and put the bags down, Gram turned the conversation away from food. "I saw Jake working on the bunkhouse. Did you know he was coming over?"

"I had no idea," Sam said. "And I'm sort of surprised he didn't come help us carry the groceries."

Gram gave a hum of agreement, then added, "I'm about to bake a yellow cake with brown sugar and toasted coconut icing. If that doesn't bring him to the house, he's not the Jake I know."

Sam opened the fresh pink-and-white box of sugar cubes and took two before hurrying back to Ace.

"A promise is a promise," she told the bay. His ears pricked up and his nostrils vibrated as she held her hand flat with the sugar cubes balanced on her palm.

His velvety lips lifted the sugar. His head bobbed, eyes closed, and he drooled a little as he savored the sweetness.

Sam petted the light patch of hair that showed where Ace had been freeze-branded. It had been years since he'd run free with the Phantom's herd, and his life was much easier on River Bend Ranch, but thinking of the way Dark Sunshine had yearned toward the range this morning made her wonder if Ace remembered freedom.

"No more," she said, when he sniffed her hand loudly. "Too much isn't good for you."

The gelding blew through his lips as if she were talking nonsense, but he went willingly back to the round corral and Sweetheart.

Sam grabbed the big bag of dog chow from Gram's truck. Balancing it against her hip, she made it back into the house.

"Give that to me," Gram said. "And you go see what's up with Jake. Go on, shoo."

"I don't want to," Sam protested. "He's mad about something. Look."

Sam and Gram stood in the doorway together. When Gram took a deep breath, Sam thought she was about to offer advice.

"I smell violets," Gram said instead.

So did Sam. The tiny flowers bloomed in the shadows near the house.

"But what about Jake?"

Gram tilted her head to one side. She tucked a strand of gray hair back toward her neat bun.

"You're right," Gram said. "He's working like a man trying to erase what's on his mind. I imagine it has something to do with Mac."

Quickly, Sam's brain sorted through all the local names she knew. Her two-year stay in San Francisco, after her accident, sometimes made it hard to remember everyone.

"Who's Mac?" she asked.

"MacArthur Ely, Jake's grandfather. I ran into Helen Coley in town and she mentioned he was visiting at Three Ponies Ranch."

"Ohhh," Sam said. She'd heard rumors about Jake's grandfather. Some said he was a shaman with special powers. Jake loudly denied that, saying his grandfather was just a Shoshone elder who respected the old ways. "But Jake likes his grandfather."

"I'm sure he does," Gram said, but her tone wavered.

"So why would he be mad that his grandfather's visiting?"

Even as she asked, Sam had a feeling she knew.

Jake's Dad was Shoshone and his mom wasn't, but Jake took no note of that from day to day. One of the quickest ways to annoy him, in fact, was to ask about his Native American heritage.

Just a few weeks ago, when Mrs. Allen had looked at the blind foal she'd rescued and remarked on its Medicine Hat markings and their significance to some tribes, Jake had grumbled.

"Go talk to him," Gram said pointedly.

"There's no way you're going to let me out of this, is there?"

"Honey, you're Jake's friend," Gram said, then disappeared toward the pantry.

Jake sat on a stump, gazing at the horses in the ten-acre corral, as Sam walked across the ranch yard.

She knew exactly how to cheer him up. He'd like being one of the first three to know about Mrs. Allen's race and he wouldn't be able to resist the lure of the grand prize.

Sam walked a little faster. She thought Jake made a jerking movement, as if he considered escaping. Maybe she was wrong, though, because he was still sitting there when she walked up.

But before she told him about the race, she'd try to find out what he was upset about. Jake hated being coddled, so Sam decided to be direct.

"What's wrong with you today?"

"Nothin'," Jake said, looking up from half-lidded eyes.

"You decided to come over and finish half the bunkhouse reconstruction all alone for no reason?"

"Just bein' neighborly," he said.

"If you were being neighborly, you would've yelled 'hi' at me and Jen."

"Didn't know you'd taken to being so sensitive," Jake began, but then a long breath whooshed between his lips. "I don't want to talk about it, okay?"

Wow. That had happened faster than she'd expected. Deciding she had nothing to lose, she asked, "Does it have to do with your grandfather?"

The look Jake flashed her made Sam think she should duck, but it faded. Jake shook his head and stared toward the mountains.

"He wants me to do some kind of a manhood initiation thing," Jake said.

A frown contracted Sam's forehead. She thought about fighting a grizzly bear, one-on-one. No. That stereotype was hundreds of years old. The instant she felt the frown, she lifted her eyebrows to erase it.

Jake couldn't mean something like that.

"Really?" she said.

Most people would take that as a cue to explain. With Jake, you never knew. She didn't get her hopes up. Living with Dad, who had the same I'll-take-care-of-it-myself personality as Jake, had prepared her for disappointment.

"Really," Jake said. "He doesn't care that I don't have time, getting ready for track season, either."

Laughter came from the carpenters who were taking their lunch break. The back door of the empty bunkhouse swung creaking in a gust of wind. Sam wished she'd grabbed her jacket when she'd come back outside. If she stayed long enough to get something out of Jake, she could be here until sundown.

"What kind of initiation thing are you talking about?"

"Grandfather doesn't care what we do. Like, it doesn't have to be Shoshone, but he says we shouldn't turn our backs on the old ways. We should master just one thing."

We. That sounded like Jake wasn't the only one. His brothers must be included, too. That sounded reasonable to Sam. Gram wanted her to learn to cook her mom's favorite recipe. Wasn't that sort of the same thing?

"So, your brothers have to do something with you?"

Jake's expression stayed blank as he said, "They've already done their stuff."

"Oh." Sam gritted her teeth together to keep from begging for more information. To her, this family custom sounded incredibly cool, but Jake still didn't want to tell her.

"You're dying for details, aren't you?" Jake said.

Sam nodded.

He sighed as if he were weary of the recitation

before he'd even begun.

"Kit went on, like, an old school vision quest. Surviving in the wild, living off the land. That sort of thing."

Sam didn't interrupt, but she wanted to know more about Kit. She knew he was Jake's oldest brother, but she'd never met him. Where did he live? How old was he? Why had he left Darton County? She knew enough to keep quiet, though.

"Nate learned to be a fancy dancer and he performed at a powwow in Reno. Adam built a canoe the old way and he still hauls it out to Monument Lake sometimes. Bryan built a sweat lodge. Dad calls it our Indian sauna. We all use it once in a while. And Quinn learned to drum. Grandfather had him play at some ceremony last fall. And then there's me.

"Mom says it's important to do something, because it will make Dad and Grandfather happy. But she can't fool me. The history teacher part of her thinks it's great.

"She brought up all these examples of family traditions, like joining your parents' church or the fraternity your dad was in at college, stuff that's a lot more of a commitment than this." Jake stopped, shaking his head. "She actually suggested I make a teepee. Can you believe it? Like Darrell—"

Jake bit off the end of the sentence, but Sam could guess what he'd been about to say. Jake's best friend Darrell didn't have to make a teepee or a canoe or a sweat lodge. Was Jake just afraid of being different?

"You wear your hair long," Sam said. Maybe pointing it out would remind him he didn't care that much if he stood out from the crowd.

"Other guys have long hair."

Not like yours, she wanted to say.

Instead, Sam turned her face skyward. The wind had vanished and the sun shone from between the clouds.

She didn't pin Jake down and ask what he was going to do. He'd already told her more than she'd expected. She was satisfied and a little flattered that he'd confided in her.

"Hey," she said. "Gram's making a cake and she wants you to come eat some of it. Think you can hang around that long?"

Jake nodded. Then, at the sound of hooves, he looked toward the rear of the ranch, past the broken barn, beyond the corrals to the path that led up the hillside and eventually to Aspen Creek.

Brynna and Dad were coming home. Their voices sounded relaxed and happy. Sam was glad, but their arrival meant an end to her talk with Jake.

Her eyes turned back to his. For a second, before he brought down the shutters of his eyelids, she saw his confusion.

She didn't say anything, of course, but something in Jake's dark-brown eyes had reminded her of this morning, and the geese she'd seen, trying to decide whether to fly with the flock or split off on their own.

Chapter Four

$\mathcal{B}$efore Sam could tell Jake about Mrs. Allen's race, Brynna and Dad trotted up, talking.

"Strawberry looks like a different horse when Dad rides her," Sam muttered to Jake.

The roan approached in a classic cow-horse jog. Usually, she looked like a plump, pouty mare who'd do anything to escape exertion. With Dad astride, Strawberry's Quarter horse breeding showed in every muscle.

"She knows he won't put up with any nonsense," Jake said. "That takes a burden off a horse, knowin' she can't be in charge."

Brynna rode River Bend's only Appaloosa. Maybe because he was shedding his winter coat, the spots on Jeepers-Creepers' gray body looked especially clear, as if he'd been splattered with black paint. He arched his neck as he approached.

Both horses seemed to be having as good a time as their riders. Seeing Brynna and Dad together, Sam couldn't stay irritated that Dad had lectured her about her inept riding. How could she complain when Dad and Brynna looked so happy?

Brynna wore a long-sleeved white blouse and her red hair was clipped into a low ponytail instead of her workday French braid. She swayed in the polished Western saddle and the one hand that didn't hold her reins fluttered in the air, punctuating her conversation.

In a pearl-snapped shirt so faded that Sam couldn't tell if it had originally been green or blue, Dad looked like his usual self. He was a cowboy through and through, tough and lean as a strip of beef jerky, with a face marked by sun and weather. But since he'd married Brynna, just before Christmas, Dad looked content most of the time.

Right now, Dad was considering the saw in Jake's hands. He looked surprised, but he didn't have a chance to ask questions.

"It seems we're having company," Brynna said as she halted the Appaloosa and swung down to the ground.

"We are?" Sam felt a little lurch of excitement. "When?"

"Few hours from now," Dad said.

Brynna laughed, holding her hands palm up as if she couldn't explain how it had happened. "I guess because it's the first nice day in a while, everyone was out for a ride. Once we'd invited the Kenworthys and Slocums, we couldn't wait to ask your family, too, Jake."

"We'll double the number of places you need at the table," Jake said.

Sam did a quick calculation. She might be weak in algebra, but she could add three Kenworthys, plus two Slocums—Rachel was in France on a two-week exchange program—and eight Elys. Oh, and she should probably count Jake's grandfather.

Before she reached a total, Dad changed the equation.

"Might as well see if Trudy and Helen wanna come, too," Dad said.

It took Sam a second to realize he meant Mrs. Allen and Helen Coley, Gram's friend who worked as a housekeeper for the Slocums. With those two, she was up to seventeen. With the River Bend cowboys and the Forster family, where would they put everyone?

"Isn't that like, twenty-four people?" Sam blurted.

Brynna and Dad laughed.

"It won't be a sit-down deal," Dad said.

"It's a potluck. Everyone will bring anything they feel like cooking. Beans, biscuits, buttermilk pie—whatever. We'll drag a table out here."

As Brynna gestured vaguely to the ranch yard, she grinned and Sam thought her stepmother looked as excited as a girl.

"And the best part," Brynna went on, "is we all have scrap wood from earthquake damage and no one's taken the time to burn it yet, so we're going to have a bonfire!"

"Cool," Jake said.

"That is *so* cool," Sam echoed, but she really meant "unbelievable."

Her predictable ranch family never did spontaneous things like this.

Dad shook his head, but his smile said it had been way too long since he'd allowed such fun.

"And Jen's coming, too?" Sam asked, just to be sure.

"Yes, in fact her family's riding over together," Brynna said.

Sam felt a glow of satisfaction. Jen's family would make a pretty picture, each riding one of the famous Kenworthy palominos. But that wasn't even the best part. Jed and Lila Kenworthy had suffered through a few tough months. Sam had feared her best friend would be forced to move away, since her parents had seemed on the verge of a divorce.

It had taken a horse to get them back together.

Rosa d'Oro wasn't yet ready to ride, so she probably wouldn't be coming to the party, but the long-lost palomino had helped mend the Kenworthy family.

"I'd better get going," Jake said, dusting off the saw blade before he set it aside.

"But I need to tell you something," Sam protested.

She had to tell Jake about Mrs. Allen's race.

"Mom will be—" Jake began.

"What about Gram's cake?" Sam tried to tempt him into staying just a little longer.

Her efforts had nothing to do with Gram's yellow cake, either. She couldn't stop thinking how cool it would be if she had a race partner right now.

She didn't want to make Jen jealous, Sam told herself sternly. But she didn't want to give Jake too long to think, either.

"Mom will be asking for everyone's help," Jake continued in spite of her interruption. "And if I'm not there, who knows what kinda chores they'll leave for me."

"I just—"

"You'll have plenty of time to talk tonight," Brynna said. She used such a candy-sweet tone, Sam knew Brynna had misinterpreted everything.

"But there's this thing . . ." Sam kept her voice calm and reasonable.

"It'll wait," Dad said.

She was getting frustrated. Dad and Brynna were going to leave her with a permanent stutter if they didn't stop cutting her off in midsentence. Come to think of it, why was it she got in trouble when *she* interrupted?

"It won't wait," Sam said. "I need—"

"For cryin' out loud, Samantha," Dad chuckled. "Let the boy go."

Jake made an amused sort of snort, but when

Sam turned to glare at him, he had the good sense to keep quiet.

Gram loved the idea of a spring celebration.

"We'll put off the lasagna lesson for today," Gram said. "It's about time there was a party around here."

Sam felt her spirits sag a little. All the talk about family traditions had her hoping a lasagna lesson would stir up memories of her mother.

She had plenty of other things to think about as she helped Gram spend the afternoon cooking.

They sprinkled salt on some things, sugar on others. They chopped and fried onions and beef for an enormous pot of chili Gram planned to keep hot on a camp stove outside.

Gram did much of her cooking with the telephone clamped between her ear and shoulder and Sam heard her give Mrs. Allen, Helen Coley, and Jake's mom all the same advice—"Just double the recipe!"

Sam and Brynna tripled the usual dinnertime salad order. They made three big wooden bowls full of salad—one green, one pasta, and another full of early spring fruit.

"I'll have to go back into town all over again on Monday," Gram said, as the supplies she'd just bought vanished under knives and into pots. "But who cares? I bought it to eat!"

By the time dusk settled, the ranch was alive with friends. Car doors opened and neighbors shouted "Hello!" Truck tailgates slammed down to release their cargo and the crack of splitting wood echoed everywhere. Planks, boards, and rafters ruined by the earthquake became a pyramid of wood for a spring bonfire.

Boots tramped across the yard and up to the white, two-story ranch house. The kitchen door opened over and over again and voices asked, "Is there room for this in the refrigerator?", and "Can I stick this in the oven?"

While Sam slathered loaves of sourdough bread with butter and garlic, she watched over her shoulder for Jen and Jake. Not that she expected either of them to come help in the kitchen, but anything was possible.

Jake's mom, who also happened to be Mrs. Ely, Sam's history teacher, bustled in and began working on a dish she called Indian tacos.

"I make it whenever Luke's dad comes to visit," Mrs. Ely said as Gram made room for her at the kitchen counter. "He says I have a knack for fry bread. Jake's supposed to be bringing the dough." She glanced toward the door. "I'd just put it out to rise when Luke came in saying he'd seen Brynna and Wyatt."

Sam smiled as she finished wrapping the loaves in aluminum foil. Jake had been afraid he'd get the left-over chores, and here he came into the kitchen, crowded with all females, carrying a cookie sheet full of dough lumps the size of small apples.

"Yeah, laugh at me," he grunted as he slipped past

Sam. "You're gonna eat your heart out when you hear Grandfather's idea."

"I will?" Sam dodged along at Jake's heels. "What is it?"

She didn't care if she looked like a bothersome puppy. "You're gonna eat your heart out" had to mean horses. She wouldn't let him ignore her.

Sam tugged on Jake's sleeve. It looked like a new shirt. Blue-gray and crisp, the shirt was nice, and she didn't care one bit.

"Tell me," she insisted.

"Later," he mumbled and started for the door.

He didn't get very far.

Ryan Slocum stood in the doorway. Politely, he bowed Mrs. Allen through ahead of him. Then he remained there, balancing a tray heaped with pink shrimp on a bed of crushed ice. He was blocking Jake's way and he made no attempt to step aside.

"'Scuse me." Jake said the words quietly, but there was a challenge in them that made Gram and Jake's mother look up.

Sam couldn't see Jake's face, but the blue-gray shirt tightened across his back. He squared his shoulders and let his arms float out an inch or so from his body.

She *could* see Ryan's face. Head tilted to one side so that the kitchen light glinted off his sleek, coffee-colored hair, he wore a mocking smile.

Sam wasn't sure why she should think such a thing, but it looked like Jake and Ryan were ready to fight.

Chapter Five

"They might as well be hounds raising their hackles," whispered Mrs. Allen as she watched the two boys.

She needn't have whispered, Sam thought. Neither guy was paying attention.

"That may be, but I won't tolerate a dogfight in my kitchen." Gram gave an exasperated sigh and moved between them. "Well thank you, Ryan." Gram whisked the tray from his hands. "I can't imagine where these came from."

"Honestly, I do not know," Ryan's British accent made him sound a bit bewildered.

"Jake, please find a place for these in the refrigerator." Gram shoved the tray of shrimp in his direction.

Sam heard Mrs. Ely smother a laugh as Jake,

frowning, accepted the tray and opened the refrigerator.

As he did, Ryan nodded, and left the crowded kitchen for the yard.

Jake wedged the tray into the refrigerator then followed after Ryan.

Gram caught Sam's eye.

Sam held her breath. Every woman in the room looked at her expectantly.

"I have no idea what that was all about," Sam admitted, waving her hands as if erasing something before her. "They just don't get along."

The women laughed and the kitchen clatter resumed.

"Go have fun and don't worry about them," Gram said, smiling.

Sam didn't have to be told twice. She wanted to know Jake's secret. Now. And grilling Jake about Ryan wouldn't help. Jake had never said straight out why he disliked Ryan. He used excuses, like his scorn for English riding.

That was a weak explanation. Jake admired all good riders.

Sam was pretty sure Jake was jealous of Ryan's easy life, but he was ashamed to admit it.

Ryan could have anything he wanted: cars, horses, vacations to the tropics. Jake saved every penny he earned. His parents poured thousands of dollars into the Three Ponies Ranch and hoped a good upbringing would put their sons on the right track. There was little left over for movies, dinners out, or even college.

Each boy had to earn what he got.

Just as she came out to the porch, three riders, shadowy in the dusk, clattered over the bridge. It had to be Jen's family.

As she moved out to meet them, Sam passed the Ely men. They stood like redwood trees around the wood piled for the bonfire, as Dad prepared to light it.

When Dad squatted near the house-high pile of firewood, Sam slowed down. She really wanted to see this. She wasn't the only one. Nearby, Pepper, River Bend's youngest cowboy, fidgeted as if he were waiting for Fourth of July fireworks.

"Shall we wait for full dark?" Dad shouted over to Luke Ely, Jake's dad.

Luke glanced toward his sons. Thumbs slung from the pockets of clean jeans, they shrugged, leaving it up to the older men.

"Plenty of fuel, there," Luke said.

Dad's broad smile said he didn't want to wait, either.

Linc Slocum, in a royal-blue shirt with fancy fringe, hovered nearby. He wore a bolo tie with a silver slide shaped like a buffalo's head. It had sparkling red eyes. A leather belt encircled his barrel-shaped body. Its buckle was cast to look like the entire body of a buffalo. This one had little green eyes.

Linc shifted from foot to foot as if his boots were too tight.

If he'd been anyone else, Sam would have

laughed. Linc Slocum looked like a comical rich guy playing cowboy, but he could be dangerous. He'd tried underhanded tricks to get the Phantom. He only wanted the stallion as a trophy, but the Phantom's silver-white neck wore a scar inflicted by Slocum years ago.

Lately, Slocum seemed to have given up on catching the stallion, but Sam didn't trust him. He considered the range his playground and cared nothing for those who called it home.

Dad glanced up in time to catch Sam's glare. He gave her an understanding smile and lifted one shoulder. Linc Slocum was a neighbor, so they put up with him.

"Ya might want to pour a little kerosene on that pile of sticks," Linc suggested. "That'd get things goin' in a hurry!"

Sam had seen one fire threaten River Bend Ranch. Linc's idea would almost guarantee another.

Luckily, everyone ignored him and, as Sam watched, streamers of orange flame began twisting through the wood. With a whoosh, the bonfire started and everyone watching clapped.

Sam rushed to help the Kenworthys with their horses. Before she reached them, she recognized the familiar smell of exercised horses and breathed deeply. Amid the aromas of homemade food, freshly washed clothes and shampoo, the scent of horses was the best perfume of all. She guessed anyone who would say that must really love horses.

"Jen!" Sam called.

All three Kenworthys turned. Their palominos looked, too. The horses had Quarter horse conformation, dark golden hides, and snowy manes and tails. Jen's Silly was the tallest and Sam knew she was nearly sixteen hands high. Jed Kenworthy's stallion Sundown and Lila's mare Mantilla were about half a hand shorter.

Just as Sam was wondering whether she should tether the three high-strung horses next to each other, Ross appeared. He was the biggest and shyest of River Bend's cowboys.

"Rails are up on the barn corral," Ross said, then looked up expectantly.

He must be waiting for the Kenworthys to swing down from their saddles, Sam decided, so he could put the palominos together in the barn corral.

As they dismounted, the palominos looked around restlessly, wondering what would happen next.

"I've got to get these, first." Lila opened her saddlebags and slid out a box. "Your Gram said we could come empty-handed, since we were riding," Lila said. "But I'd just finished dipping some chocolates."

"Wow," Sam said. She could imagine the candy melting on her tongue.

"Don't open them," Jen cautioned her mother. "You'll make Sam drool."

Sam gave Jen a shove and Jen pushed back, but they both stopped when they realized Ross was still waiting.

When the Kenworthys had turned over their reins, Ross nodded and trudged away.

"Thanks," Lila called after him.

Jed turned to Sam, shook his head, and said, "He's still as a stone wall."

"That's probably the last we'll see of him for a while," Sam agreed. It was actually kind of funny that Jed noticed. He was almost as quiet as Ross.

While the adults walked ahead, Jen took off her ponytail holder and ran her fingers through her hair. Ripply and white blond, it glowed as they neared the bonfire. But Jen looked so self-conscious, Sam hesitated to tell her she looked nice. Jen would deny she'd gone to some extra trouble for Ryan.

Then Sam thought of something she *could* say.

"Hey, you really want to win, don't you?" Sam asked. When Jen looked surprised, she added, "You look great."

Jen flushed, then put on a fake drawl. "Yep, I'm going to get me a partner, one way or t'other."

Giggling, they passed through the crowd of neighbors. They edged past Mrs. Coley as she explained her recipe for fresh salsa and whispered that it was like a vacation with Rachel out of town. They watched Bryan and Adam Ely sit on the edge of the porch to tune their guitars. They took the hot pink paper flyers Mrs. Allen handed them with a wink.

THE SUPER BOWL OF HORSEMANSHIP the brochure announced in big block letters. The outline of a running horse was centered just beneath it. It looked almost like a photograph, and as she noticed that, Sam remembered Mrs. Allen was an artist.

The rest of the flyer was worded just like the draft she and Jen had read. The only thing that was different was the entry fee, printed clearly at the very bottom.

Sam thought again of how hard Jake worked and how much he'd love to win money for a new truck.

"All I have to do is show this to him . . ." Jen was looking down at the flyer and muttering when she collided with Jake.

"Watch where you're—" Jen began, but when she noticed Jake wasn't alone, she apologized. "Sorry!"

Next to Jake stood a man who must be his grandfather, MacArthur Ely.

He looked just like Luke, Jake's dad. He had the same angled cheekbones and the same healthy bronze skin. The lines around his mouth swooped back toward his jawline, carved there by a customary half smile.

Only two things about him were really different. He had steel-gray hair trimmed into a crew cut, and an expression that showed where Jake had gotten his lively mustang eyes.

Before Jake could introduce his grandfather, Jen bolted.

"Nice to see you again, Mr. Ely. I'm sorry," she said breathlessly, and gestured across the bonfire. Sam would bet Jen had seen Ryan and wanted to get him as her partner before anyone else did.

Mr. Ely clearly didn't mind Jen's quick exit. He smiled after her, seemed to listen to a few bars of strumming from his other grandsons' guitars, then faced Sam. He met her eyes as if he knew her.

"Samantha Forster, I haven't seen you since you were seven years old."

He didn't tell her she'd grown or changed or any of the obvious things adults usually said as they shook your hand. In fact, he didn't even shake her hand, exactly.

Sam jumped when Jake's grandfather enclosed her hand in both of his. He held it a second, as if warming it. His palms were surprisingly soft considering that the back of his hands were scuffed and rough from work.

Seven years old. Her mom had died that year, but Sam didn't ask if Mr. Ely had seen her before or after her mom's death.

"You have your mother's heart for animals, I'm told." Mr. Ely's smile didn't look sad. "And I can see you have her eyes."

"And Jake has yours, Mr. Ely," Sam answered. It was a brash thing to say and Sam had no idea where she'd gotten the courage. It had just popped out.

"Call me Mac."

"Thanks," Sam said.

Jake began shifting and looking at the noisy group around the bonfire as if Sam ought to go join them, and Sam realized she'd been staring at the old man. Would he think she was rude?

If so, he must be used to it. Mac Ely looked like a blend of the old West and the new.

He wore modern boots and jeans, but his soft chamois-colored flannel shirt draped over him like deerhide.

"I want to show you a horse," Mac said suddenly.

"Me?" Sam asked. There really didn't seem to be any question that Jake's grandfather was addressing her, but she snatched a quick look at Jake just the same. Jake stared at Mac as if he wanted to ask the same question.

Mac nodded. "The horse is for Jake. She's running free on tribal lands and he will catch her."

Sam's pulse hummed with excitement. Canoes and sweat lodges were fine, but this was more like it. Capturing a free-roaming horse would be the kind of challenge she'd like.

Jake smiled, but he looked more resigned than excited.

"Where is she?" Sam asked.

Brynna had told her that the Bureau of Land Management and local tribes sometimes clashed over horses. If mustangs ran on tribal lands, they were governed by a different set of laws than if they lived on public lands. A little line on a map could make a big difference.

"One finger of tribal land stretches east between Lost Canyon and Arroyo Azul," Jake said. "On the other side of the mountains there's a high desert lake."

"Monument Lake," Sam said. "Isn't that it?"

Mac nodded. "That's home to the tribe's horses."

She hadn't been there since she'd returned from San Francisco, but Sam had a vague memory of a lake set like a turquoise stone in the sage and sand desert. She imagined horses running there and felt chills. It would be beautiful.

Suddenly, she wondered if Mac knew how good his grandson was with horses. Catching one, even a wild one, wouldn't be that hard for him.

"Has she been ridden before?" Sam asked.

"Not successfully," Mac said.

Oh boy, this just kept getting better and better!

"'Ain't a horse that can't be rode,'" Jake said, quoting an old saying, but Sam knew the rest of the rhyme.

"'Ain't a cowboy that can't be throwed.'"

Mac smiled, indulging them.

"Jake will catch her and run her in the race," Mac said.

"I will?" Jake was clearly surprised by the second half of his grandfather's statement. "The race is soon. If I caught her tomorrow, even counting in spring vacation, which would help, I'd only have two weeks to work with her."

"What do you do that's hard?" Mac asked, and his solemn voice stopped everything.

All at once, Sam felt like an outsider. Jake's world and his grandfather's had shrunk to just the two of them. Mac's head jerked just slightly to one side, silencing Jake before he said something defensive.

"Think before you speak," Mac ordered. "Then tell me what you do that's so hard you're not sure you can succeed?"

Jake's eyelids drooped and he went still. His grandfather's words hadn't shamed him. He was really thinking.

Sam did the same. Studying made good grades possible. Daily attention to everything she set down made her room stay neat. Meeting her friends' and family members' eyes each time they spoke to her made communication lots easier. The only thing she needed to really work on was convincing Dad—and herself—she could ride.

As a wave of warmth gusted from the bonfire to surround her, Sam had a feeling that not even *that* was really out of reach.

Jake must have come to a similar conclusion.

"Not that much," he said at last.

Mac nodded. "Before I pass over, I want to know my son's sons can handle the heart-busting days that will come."

Had her flesh just hugged tighter to her bones? Sam shivered. Mac didn't look sick, but when he said, "Before I pass over," could he be talking about anything but dying?

Whatever he meant, his satisfied smile said he was pleased with Jake's response.

Suddenly the world expanded again, to include Sam, the wooden table full of food, and the other guests.

Sam heard Ryan's British accent and saw him standing near Jen. She smelled burned sugar and saw a marshmallow on a stick go up in flames.

"We'll come for you at five o'clock," Mac said.

"In the morning?" Sam gasped. Of course she wanted to go. There was no way she'd turn down the chance to see the tribe's herd. But five o'clock . . .

"In the morning," Mac repeated. Then his head lifted as if he'd heard something.

Sam noticed a flurry of movement around Linc Slocum. Part of her didn't want to know what he was up to, but Gram's familiar voice carried to her. Sam couldn't make out the exact words of their conversation, but she'd bet Slocum was presenting another of his money-making schemes.

What would it be this time? He'd tried to hoodwink the BLM by having an employee infiltrate their group of wranglers. He'd worked with an unscrupulous rodeo contractor to use his Brahma bulls in exchange for help in trapping wild horses. And he'd tried to bait mustangs into grazing by the road so they'd look picturesque to potential investors in his guest ranch.

Apparently she wasn't the only one who wanted to eavesdrop, because the conversations around the bonfire grew so hushed, Sam could hear Gram's voice.

"What will you do with them, Linc?" Gram asked.

"Not exactly sure, ma'am. Could be I'll raise them like beef, or maybe keep 'em penned on my place to hunt. Not for myself, you understand, but for those dudes who've never been closer to one than a restaurant buffalo burger."

Buffalo?

Linc snickered as if he'd made a great joke.

"First I've heard of it," mumbled Jed Kenworthy, who stood nearby with Lila, Dad, and Brynna.

Sam's mind spun, trying to catch up.

Then Brynna stepped into the circle of firelight. Though she wore a long denim skirt and pink blouse, she moved with the firm assurance that went with her uniform.

Dad turned to Jed and muttered, "Hang onto your hats."

"Linc," Brynna said conversationally, "hunting bison wouldn't be all that sporting, would it?"

Sam didn't know the answer to that, and when her neighbors glanced at each other with raised eyebrows, she didn't think they did, either. The high desert wasn't buffalo country.

"I just liked the look of 'em," Linc said, shrugging.

A few people chuckled, but in the seconds of silence that followed as they waited for the skirmish to continue, Sam heard her best friend's laughter. Then came Jen's voice, as clear as if she'd used a microphone.

"Honestly, that would be just like hunting cows!"

Sam knew Jen hated being the center of attention, but she'd attracted all eyes anyway. Worst of all, Linc Slocum stared directly at her as if she were about to be sorry.

Chapter Six

Jen's hand flew up to cover her mouth, but clearly everyone had heard. Though several neighbors muttered their agreement, Sam was amazed.

Jen was levelheaded and logical. Usually. But she was standing there, talking to Ryan. Her words made it clear she thought Linc Slocum was either stupid or unscrupulous. Even if she was right, Linc was Ryan's dad.

Slocum gave a humorless chuckle and shook his finger toward Jen. "There you go chattering just like my girl. But you probably haven't heard they're pretty fierce. And for just the skull and cape," he made a gesture that included the top of his head and down to his shoulders. "Some hunting ranches are getting two or three thousand dollars. More than that, if you let the customer keep the meat."

Sam felt queasy. Linc didn't sound like a man who'd bought bison just because he "liked the look of them."

Beside her, Jed and Mac stood with crossed arms. Their faces were expressionless and she wished they'd say something.

"You want to be sure and have them tested before you put them out on the range," cautioned Mrs. Allen. "I was reading about some trouble they had in Montana with beefalo— the crossbred, you know— carrying disease."

"Probably I'll keep them penned with my Brahmas—"

"Ain't that gonna be a hoot," Jed muttered.

"—but thanks for your advice," Linc's tight-jawed response signaled he didn't sound grateful at all. He looked around, waiting for laughter, but his sarcasm fell flat.

Trudy Allen might be an artist and sort of eccentric, but she'd lived in Darton County for years and her husband had been a respected cattleman. No one would side with Linc against her.

Sam chanced a glance toward Ryan and Jen. Jen met Sam's eyes with a pleading look Sam couldn't interpret. Ryan just looked embarrassed.

She couldn't say exactly why he did, because everyone standing near the fire wore a red cast from the flames. It was something in the way he held his shoulders, tense and immobile.

"Well now, maybe we'll think of some way to show off my buffalo and help publicize your Super Bowl of Horsemanship at the same time," Linc tried to pluck the pink flyer from the pocket of gabardine pants that were way too tight. It took a few minutes, but finally he pinched an edge of the pink paper and slid it free. "Don't ya think people would like to look over an authentic herd of wild buffalo while they're waiting for my son to win the race?"

Ryan didn't waste another moment on embarrassment. He knew people would start talking if he didn't.

"You flatter me, Father." Somehow the words were audible, though Ryan spoke through gritted teeth. "There are many more talented riders here—"

"Oh, knock off the false modesty, boy. You're a top-notch rider and Sky Ranger's in prime condition for a race. They might know the lay of the land better, but that only means you use one of them for a partner."

Use one of them. Sam shook her head. Linc Slocum must not realize his words almost guaranteed no one would want to ride with Ryan.

Then Slocum winked at Jen and Sam knew she was wrong. Jen would ride with Ryan. She wondered how Silly would do, though. Jen's palomino was strong. Sam had never seen her falter a single step, no matter the terrain or length of the ride. But Mrs. Allen's flyer would be sure to attract many other riders. Did Silly have the temperament to run with a field of competitive horses?

"I guess no one's going to finish these tacos or eat this cake," Gram's mock despair cut across the uneasy silence. "What's a person to think when there's an entire yellow layer cake just going to waste? I guess maybe I should whistle for the dog and see if he'll eat it."

Five minutes later, Mac had managed to snag fry bread for himself and Sam, and pile it high with taco meat, lettuce, and cheese, before he rejoined his son and daughter-in-law. Jake had filled a bowl with shrimp and dipping sauce. Now he and Sam leaned against the hitching rail, quietly watching the party go on.

Most guests were licking icing from their lips, and the cake plate was empty. Adam and Bryan were playing a rollicking song on their guitars while someone sang along. Sam was so sure the mellow mood would last until everyone had gone home, she didn't jinx it by asking Jake what he thought of Linc's buffalo scheme.

She only felt a twinge of worry when Jen and Ryan approached.

Jake muttered, "Here comes trouble."

Sam elbowed him in reprimand.

"Think how embarrassed he must be," she whispered.

Jake answered with an unsympathetic grunt.

"Hi," Jen said, a little too cheerily.

"Hi," Sam responded. She was still wondering what to say next when Ryan spoke up.

"So, Ely, you'll be riding in this race, I suppose?"

"Sure," Jake said. "And you?"

Ryan shrugged. "I'm sure that big black mare of yours is up to it."

Silence filled in behind Ryan's statement, which somehow sounded like a question. After a few seconds, Sam couldn't stand the tension.

"He might not be riding Witch," she said, and then Jake's glare stabbed her and the word *mistake* repeated again and again in her brain, ringing out like a burglar alarm.

"Really?" Jen asked. "Which horse are you going to ride?"

"Uh," Sam said, looking to Jake for help.

Jake smiled back at her, but his grin didn't hold an ounce of friendliness. *You got us into this*, his expression said, *now get us out*.

Sam noticed Jen watching her, trying to offer support. She knew Jake was blaming Sam for speaking up.

"That big chocolate horse of your brother's, perhaps?" Ryan asked.

"Naw," Jake said.

Sam knew Jake wouldn't let her off the hook. Jen knew it, too, but Ryan kept guessing.

"That red chestnut," he said, looking at the ten-acre pasture.

"Nike's really only good over short distances," Sam said, but she knew the distraction wasn't working.

"I give up," Ryan said.

"He'll be riding one of the Shoshone horses," Sam said.

"From out at Monument Lake?" Jen pounced on Sam's words with excitement. "Are they in shape? The graze is sparse out there and it's been a hard winter."

As Jen's voice trailed off, Sam could almost hear her friend wondering if the harsh conditions would lead to a stronger horse or an unhealthy one.

Ryan passed one hand over his sleek hair and exhaled loudly.

"You're riding a wild horse, then?"

"Guess so," Jake said.

For the first time since her blunder, Jake seemed to be enjoying himself. He wasn't gloating, exactly, but Sam recognized that lazy tomcat smile. He knew the announcement had aroused Ryan's competitive spirit.

"You're convinced you can have a wild horse ready to compete in just two weeks." Ryan wasn't asking a question, he was deciding whether it was possible.

"That's a pretty big job, even for you," Jen said.

"She won't have to do anything fancy; just run where I point her."

Mrs. Coley arrived with a pan full of brownies,

begging them to eat. They did, but the conversation about horses wasn't over and they all knew it.

"So you'll be riding a true Indian pony," Ryan mused.

"She runs with the tribal herd. I don't know how big she'll be."

"You haven't even seen her yet?" Jen gasped. Her mouth stayed open for a moment. She used her forefinger to push her glasses back up her nose before she looked at Sam. "Is he suicidal or something?"

"It's just sort of a challenge," Sam said.

"Indeed it is," Ryan said, and then he nodded a couple times more than was normal. "I've been spending a bit of time at the Blind Faith Mustang Sanctuary. Perhaps I'll see if I can borrow one of her mustangs for the race."

"Oh my gosh," Jen said, drawing each word out. "I get it. This is turning into 'anything you can do, I can do better,' isn't it?"

"Neither of us is that juvenile, Jennifer," Ryan said, but he didn't take his eyes from Jake's.

"Yeah, Jennifer," Jake echoed.

"Wait," Sam said. "I know those horses, Ryan, and you don't have much to choose from. There's Faith's mother. She's a great horse, but still nursing. There's a sickle-hocked bay, another bay with a ewe neck. They might settle down for you," Sam said dubiously. "That little sorrel is beautiful, but her legs." Sam shook her head at the memory. "That permanently cranky black and that tiny paint with the allergic condition—forget it."

"Actually, you've forgotten the horse I'm thinking about."

"The liver chestnut who thinks he's still a stallion," Jake said.

"Indeed," Ryan said. "Mrs. Allen is calling him Roman because of his rather dramatic nose."

Sam remembered. The liver chestnut had led the "unadoptable" mustangs down the hill from Willow Springs adoption center. He'd stayed up front, too, until they reached Deerpath Ranch. She couldn't remember his conformation well enough to decide whether it was suitable for the race.

"He has the attitude to win," Sam allowed. "But that attitude is going to get you pitched off plenty before he accepts a rider."

"Well then there's a first time for everything, I suppose," Ryan said.

He wouldn't sound so unconcerned if he'd crashed into the ground face- or seat- or even shoulder-first, Sam thought. That reeling, helpless feeling was nothing to shrug off.

"Jen, we're riding out," Jed Kenworthy called.

"Why are we always the first to leave?" Jen whined, but her father continued striding toward the barn corral where Ross had turned out their horses.

While Jake and Ryan stood sizing each other up, Lila pulled the girls aside.

"The party's breaking up," Lila said, "and we'd like to get across the bridge and on our way before the cars start stampeding out of here."

It made sense to Sam, but Jen had to try for a little more time.

"Right, Mom," Jen sighed. "Just when things are getting interesting."

"Five more minutes," Lila said. "I'll saddle Silly and have her waiting for you."

"She only does that to make me feel guilty," Jen said as she watched her mother hurry after her father. Then she grabbed Sam's shirt and hauled her close enough to whisper in her ear. "Have you noticed neither of these two jerks has given a thought to the fact that they need a partner?"

"Arrogant, bigheaded creeps," Sam agreed. "They think they can just whistle and some girls will agree to ride with them." Before she went on, though, she noticed Jen watching the guys again.

"You've never been thrown from a horse?" Jake was asking incredulously.

In a flash of memory, Sam recalled arriving home after two years in San Francisco. Her first glimpse of Jake, after all that time, was his blurred form sailing over a horse's ears and landing in a swirl of dust.

"Never," Ryan confirmed, but Jake wasn't buying it.

"No horse ever stopped before a jump and you kept going? Not one ever took off when you just had one boot in the stirrup?"

"Actually, both of those have happened. I've just been fortunate enough not to have fallen."

Jake rubbed the back of his neck and stared off into the darkness. A slow smile curved his lips as if he was looking into the future and what he saw coming amused him.

"What I figure is, you just haven't been challengin' yourself, pardner," Jake said with a phony drawl.

Sam wanted to shriek when Jake pulled that fake cowpoke twang, but apparently Ryan was ready for it.

"Yeah?" he asked, with little trace of his British accent. "Well I just reckon we'll see, won't we, *pardner*?"

Chapter Seven

Sam sat straight up in bed.

Cougar mewed a complaint and jumped down. With each tiny thud of paw on hardwood floor, her dreams fell away more completely.

Sam stared through the darkness toward her bedroom doorway. Something out there had moved.

"I didn't mean to wake you. You've got about twenty more minutes to sleep," Dad whispered. "On my way down to make coffee, I just looked in to make sure you were covered up. Sometimes it gets sorta chilly toward dawn."

Sam sighed and pulled her blankets up over her shoulders.

"I'll be down when my alarm . . ." A yawn muffled

the end of her sentence.

She closed her eyes, but her brain kept churning. What had she been searching for in her dream? She couldn't remember.

The Phantom. She'd dreamed of chasing the Phantom.

Sam wiggled down lower in her bed, contented and warm. Oh, how easily she and Jake would win the race if she rode a mustang stallion and he galloped alongside on a wild Indian pony.

But she'd been looking for something more.

Sam's fingers touched her wrist and she knew. Her horsehair bracelet, braided from strands of the Phantom's silvery mane, was missing. When had she worn it last?

Mikki, the girl who'd piloted the Horse and Rider Protection Program at River Bend, had borrowed it for a little while, but she'd sent it back. Sam was sure she'd worn it since the Phantom's disappearance because he'd noticed it, that day he'd let her ride him. That wonderful day.

She swung her legs out of bed, turned on her bedside lamp, and donned the clothes she'd laid out the night before. Dressed, except for her boots, she pushed her bangs out of her eyes and started searching. She opened each of her drawers and slid her hands under her folded clothes. She closed her eyes, hoping her fingertips would be more sensitive without sight to guide them.

She found nothing in any of her clothes drawers.

Hands on hips, she turned and stared at her room. Silently, she demanded it give up its secrets. When the room wasn't intimidated by her brain waves, she kept searching. It was not on the shelf with her model horses. Not on the bookcase. It wasn't on her desk or in the blue mug she used to hold pencils and pens.

In the top right-hand desk drawer she had a few keepsakes. A gold-colored tin button box that her mother had used when she was sewing. A ribbon from the bridle she'd first used on Blackie, long before he'd grayed into the Phantom. The glossy red-brown feather she'd found on the desert floor on the day she'd watched the Phantom run free after his awful rodeo captivity.

She picked up the feather and smoothed it through her fingers. One day, she and Jen had followed a red-tailed hawk, hoping she'd drop a feather in time for Jake's birthday. She'd wanted to give it to him along with the split-ear headstall.

It hadn't happened that day, or on the day she'd heard the hawk's rasping cry and spotted it when she was riding with Jake. It had been a blustery, stormy day, the day he'd broken his leg, but he'd told her hawks were supposed to carry hopes and prayers to the sky spirits and bring back blessings.

But the hawk hadn't dropped the feather that day, either. She'd waited until Sam needed assurance that the Phantom wouldn't forget her.

Sam jumped as her alarm went off. She dropped the feather back in her desk drawer, slammed it closed, hit the "off" switch on her clock, and waited for her heart to settle down.

Four-thirty. Time to go downstairs and, as much as the idea grossed her out, eat. Dad had insisted she have breakfast before she go, or she wouldn't be allowed to leave the house. It wasn't a very hard choice.

Sam picked up her boots and stood in her doorway. She gave her mind one more chance to reveal the bracelet.

"It's not like it's magic." In a hushed voice, she belittled her own streak of superstition that just wouldn't go away.

But she and Jake would be in wild horse country. Even though Monument Lake wasn't the Phantom's usual territory, she might see him. He might sense that she wore the bracelet, a token he'd given freely.

It didn't make sense, but neither did the link she had with the wild stallion who had once been her sweet colt, Blackie.

"Samantha," Dad's whisper carried up the stairs, so Sam went.

She'd find the bracelet later.

Cougar seemed determined to trip her on the stairs. He hopped down two steps, then back up, down one more, then ran between her ankles. Once, she couldn't avoid stepping on his little tail with her stockinged feet and he gave such a tremendous screech, Blaze woofed and came rushing to the kitten's rescue.

"You three plan on wakin' everyone up early?"

Dad asked as Sam came into the kitchen.

"Blame them," Sam said, pointing at the animals before she settled into her chair at the kitchen table and began pulling on her boots.

Dad had made her milky coffee with lots of sugar and two pieces of buttered sourdough toast.

"It's too much," Sam said, sipping the hot drink.

"You don't know these old timers like Mac," Dad said, taking a drink of his own black coffee. "I do. They figure if horses only eat morning and night, that's all they need. That can be hard on you kids."

Sam laughed. "Isn't that what we did on the cattle drive? Ate a big breakfast, dinner, and nothing in between?"

"Not the same thing at all," Dad said. "You carried jerky and string cheese in your saddlebags. That and canteen water makes a fine lunch."

Sam ate a piece of toast, noticing he'd put on a lot more butter than Gram usually did. She licked her finger, then asked, "Do you know why Mac wants me to go along?"

"Don't you want to go?" Dad lowered his coffee cup slowly toward the table.

"Yes, of course. It just seems like something he'd want to do with Jake alone, though, doesn't it?"

Blaze's toenails scrambled on the linoleum as he bolted toward the kitchen door. He pressed his black nose at the crack between the door and its frame, then sniffed loud and long.

Seconds later, a car bumped over the River Bend

bridge. Sam bounded up out of her chair.

"Finish it," Dad said, pointing at a last triangle of toast.

She groaned, did as she was told, then grabbed her fleece-lined leather jacket and brown Stetson and stepped outside.

Although the sky was starting to lighten, Dad turned on the front porch light.

Jake's grandfather drove a battered red Scout. Shaped like a square Jeep, it looked like it had suffered a patchy sunburn.

When Dad chuckled, Sam could see his breath on the frosty air.

"Old troublemaker," he said, pointing at the rear of the car. Just to the right of the trailer hitch was a bumper sticker that read, "Columbus Didn't Find America; It Was Never Lost."

Sam gave a surprised laugh. She loved Mac Ely's spirit. How could Jake think he was "weird"?

Sam climbed into the backseat as Dad went around to talk with Mac at the driver's side window.

"Expect us between noon and dark," Mac told Dad. "Early enough to do that 'forgotten' homework."

Sam sighed and Jake gave a faint shake of his head. She guessed he'd long since decided it wasn't worth the effort to try to convince adults it really was possible to forget you had homework until Sunday night.

"Have fun," Dad said.

"Sure, boss," Jake replied.

"Bye," Sam called, but then Dad tilted his head so that he could see inside the vehicle.

"And be careful," Dad aimed this at Sam and though she smiled and waved, she wished he hadn't said it.

All the same, neither Jake nor Mac mentioned it.

Once Jake grumbled that he should have put in a ten-mile run to train for track today, but after that, they rode in silence down the dark highway. When their headlights flashed on a sign announcing their arrival on tribal lands Mac slowed down, cut the steering wheel hard left, and bounced onto a dirt road. After a few minutes of driving, Mac stopped the Scout to shift it into four-wheel-drive mode. It seemed to be a struggle.

"Something you'll want to remember," Mac said, grunting a little as some mechanical grinding happened inside the car, "is to baby this transmission."

Jake sat up a little straighter. "Yeah?"

"You'll need to borrow it, I think, for the days before the race. For going back and forth to watch the horse." He made a gesture with one hand as the truck bucked into gear. Then he drove on.

Jake nodded. Because it was Jake who'd taught her much of what she knew about horses, Sam understood, too. Without instructing him to do it, Mac was hinting that Jake should watch the horse for a few days before trying to capture her. Once he knew her fears and habits and hiding places, catching her would be much easier.

"The horses are on fifty fenced acres of tribal land. Kind of shaped like an old-fashioned keyhole. We go in up here," Mac gestured. "This entrance is for tribe only. And guests," he added, smiling at Sam. "Those who get special licenses to fish here, go to the other end of the lake."

"If it's fenced, how do the horses get onto BLM land? I keep hearing about it," Jake said.

"Monument Lake is shallow and warm. If a horse should take it into her head to cross to the public area, she could escape."

It was nearly light when Mac crested a rise, turned the key off, and coasted to the right-hand shoulder of the road instead of following it downhill.

Were they there? Did this mean he was sneaking up on the wild horses?

He pointed past Jake, and Sam, in the backseat, scooted all the way to the passenger's side of the truck. With her nose almost touching the window, she could see that the shoulder dropped off to thin air. Down below, Sam saw Monument Lake. They were directly above the lake's western shore, so close she could see a gull preening on a boulder.

Early morning mist veiled the lake's surface, turning the turquoise water she remembered into a pale blue blur.

But the blur wasn't still. Off to the right it swirled and parted with some sort of movement. Sam held her breath, afraid of fogging up the window and missing something.

As she watched, wind rearranged the mist and showed a band of horses. Counting quickly, she made out ten. Endless ripples curved out from the heads lowered to drink, making waves for a flotilla of gulls not far off shore.

On a slight rise of earth, one bay horse stood alone. He was their lookout, maybe the stallion, and he remained statue still. Only his mane moved on the breeze.

The horses were small and lean, mostly shades of brown. There was a single dun, with rusty markings on his face and long legs. Was that the one Mac wanted for Jake? Or could it be the broad-chested sorrel raising her head with flared nostrils, studying the ridge where the car sat in silence?

No. All at once, a black-and-white pinto splashed into the lake. One or two horses drew their muzzles from the water, annoyed. The gulls took wing, cutting white across the sky. The pinto pawed the lake's surface and shook her variegated mane as water flew up at her face. Then she stared into the wind.

"Her?" Jake asked. The word was little more than a breath, but Sam heard him.

"Her," Mac confirmed. "Yours for the taking."

Chapter Eight

"She could run," Jake said with conviction. He spoke quietly and never took his eyes from the filly. "What do you think? She's about fifteen hands? A little less?"

"Yeah," Sam said, though she didn't know if he'd been addressing her or Mac. She almost thought Jake was talking to himself.

"Compact body, deep through the heart with strong quarters. Boy, look at those muscles. And with those sloping shoulders and pasterns . . ."

"A smooth ride," Mac said, nodding. "Big eyes, light bones, and she knows rough terrain and rocky footing already."

"So why doesn't she belong to anyone?" Jake

asked. "She can't be that hard to ride."

"Maryann Pete owned her mother, a horse called Songbird. Maryann had her grandson living with her and the two of them raised this filly until she was a yearling. Then, the whole family, Maryann and her children and grandchildren, moved to Minnesota."

Sam couldn't help shivering. Nevada got cold sometimes, but she couldn't imagine living in Minnesota.

"So they turned her out before they left," Mac said, "and no one's had her until Shan Stonerow the horse breaker. You know him?"

Jake took a deep breath, gave a disapproving sound, then nodded. Mac continued.

"He had her in for a week last summer. Quick and dirty is the way he breaks horses. Catch on Monday, sell on Friday." Mac gave a snort. "She was too smart for him. He hated getting bucked off. He got mad, threw her on the ground and kept her there, tied. Idea was to make her terrified. Show her she was helpless. It didn't work."

Sam watched the filly move along the shoreline. Her markings were clear-cut, totally black and startling white. Her coat looked so satiny smooth, Sam wanted to touch it.

Mac's story made her admire the filly's fierce spirit, but the pinto's experience with the horse breaker would make her wary.

Horses trusted until you gave them a reason not

to, and the pinto had learned that not all humans were kind. How could Jake change the filly's mind?

"How did he catch her?" Jake asked. He was rubbing his palms together lightly, a gesture Sam had never seen him make before.

"Water trap," Mac said. "Even though she's playing in the water now, get her in a confined area and she'll remember, believe me."

Jake nodded. He looked hypnotized.

Just then, a car drove by and the Scout shuddered at its passing.

Inside, the car was crowded with men and fishing poles. By the time they reappeared down below, the horses had moved off, trotting single file, around the far side of Monument Lake.

"What do you think, Samantha?" Mac asked.

Sam pulled her coat closer. Without the heater running, it had grown cold in the car. Until now, she hadn't even noticed.

Mac turned away from the steering wheel and rested his arm on the seat. "Do you think Jake can tame her?"

"I think," she said slowly, "if it's not love at first sight, Jake doesn't have a chance."

Jake twisted in his seat. His lips were pressed in a hard line and his eyes were resentful.

"Why did you bring her?" Jake asked. "She wants to believe animals and humans are the same."

"I don't think they're the same," Sam protested. "They're just not that different. She's probably not friendly to humans right now, so you have to convince her you're not like Shan Stonerow or she won't give you a chance."

Mac met her eyes with a nod and Jake noticed. His resentment was easy to see. He didn't like his grandfather siding with her.

"No offense, Sam," Jake said, pretending an understanding tone, "but you're not the world's greatest horsewoman."

"I know that, *Jake*."

She also knew his words meant he wouldn't choose her as his partner. Tears burned beneath her eyelids but she refused to cry in front of him.

"Excuse me," she said, opening the car door. She held it with her shoulder, fighting the stiff morning breeze as she grabbed her Stetson off the seat. "It's a little stuffy in here. I need to get out for a minute."

The wind snatched the door away from her.

Great. They probably thought she'd slammed it in a fit of temper. Oh well, that was better than sitting there, crying. She'd rather be thought a brat than a baby.

A path led down the hillside to the lake. She took it, thinking she should have worn hiking boots or even tennis shoes instead of her slick-soled riding boots. Just the same, she didn't lose her footing.

She sat on a gray boulder, buttoned her coat to her chin and pulled her old brown Stetson down. No one would be able to see her eyes.

The rock was freezing cold through the seat of

her jeans, but that was just what she needed. Shock therapy. She blinked. Amazingly, her tears had evaporated or retracted or something. They were gone, so she could go back to the car. Quick fix. Perfect.

Not quick enough, though. A rush of falling gravel made her turn. Jake and Mac were coming down after her.

Jake was a few steps ahead of his grandfather. His jacket, a lot like hers, was open over a brick-colored tee shirt. He must be freezing.

She hoped so. She wondered how long it took for hypothermia to set in. Maybe she should stall and keep him down here for a while.

Sam stood, hands on hips. "Ready to go?" she snapped.

Jake looked up from watching his boots navigate the trail. He stood still. His hair wasn't tied back like it usually was and the wind tossed it around with such fury, for a minute he reminded her of the bay stallion who'd been here standing statue still with only his mane blowing in the wind. Through it, he met her eyes.

Jake and his stupid mustang eyes. He could just forget it if he thought she'd forgive him. What he'd said had hurt. Worse than that, he'd meant it.

He reached out and grabbed the nape of her neck.

For a second she thought he was going to push her into the lake. Instead, he gave her neck a squeeze. It pulled her hair a little and his hand was cold.

But Jake said, "Sorry."

That probably meant he didn't intend to drown her, but she just answered with a shrug. If he thought he was getting off that easy he was dreaming.

"Grandfather wants to tell you a story," Jake announced.

"I'm telling both of you," Mac said as he led the way to a rocky overhang that formed a shallow cave facing the lake. "My grandson isn't sure how to feel about his heritage. Or a lot of things."

Mac stared at Sam, as if underlining his words.

Jake blushed and hunched his shoulders forward.

"I already apologized," he told Mac, and Sam thought he sounded like a little boy.

When Mac's gaze turned to her, Sam gave a half smile. Good thing he didn't ask us to shake hands or kiss and make up, Sam thought, because she would have had to refuse, and she really liked Mac.

He gestured them into the shallow cave. The rock was bone white and it had absorbed the little morning heat there was to gather.

"This is a horse story," Mac said as he and Jake sat, too. "From the old times before there were horses."

With that puzzling beginning, Mac started his story.

"In the early days when all people lived together, the land lay in darkness. The chiefs of the world—the Hopi and Navajo, Aleut and Shoshone, whites and blacks—decided each tribe should have a place of its own. After much talk and prayer, it came to them that the people should set out walking through the darkness toward Dawnland, where the Sun and Moon lived together. If two such different beings could live in harmony, they would know how to give each tribe its proper home.

"The chiefs believed that when the first searcher reached Dawnland, Moon would give them a sign, a star shower that could be seen far and wide. The sign would tell all people to stop. In the place where they saw the star shower, they would know they were home.

"When the people set off, each tribe was determined to reach Dawnland first, but as Sun rose and set, and Moon rose and set, they realized it would take many days and they prepared to move slowly, but surely, toward their goal.

"Now, White Woman—in some tribes she's called White Shell Woman or Buffalo Calf Woman—was less patient than the rest. As she was crossing the playa, she stopped. Bending with Sun hot on her back, she scooped up three fingers full of moon-white alkali mud and molded it into a horse. It didn't matter that it was the world's first horse. She knew what to do. She vaulted instantly onto Horse's back and galloped toward Dawnland.

"When she reached it, far ahead of the others, stars showered down. Because all people were watching the sky, they saw a thousand silver flashes in the black sky. Each tribe saw the star shower. Each tribe stopped where it was meant to stop and made camp in its new home.

"Of course, White Woman paid for her impatience by having to live where it was hottest by day and coldest by night, but she remained friends with Horse and all her descendants forever after."

"I love that story," Sam said, clapping. "Is it Shoshone?"

"My daughter-in-law would tell you no."

"Being a history teacher and all," Jake said, "Mom has tried to research the roots of Grandfather's stories and they're kind of . . . elusive."

"If I borrow from many tribes' stories and blend them," Mac said, indifferently, "does it make them less true?"

Jake narrowed his eyes against the glare gathering on the lake's surface, and let Sam think about it.

Newspaper reporters got different angles on a story from different sources they interviewed, Sam thought. So did the police, when they talked with different witnesses to an event. And Gram said different books of the Bible told the same stories over again from the perspectives of different writers.

"I think it works," Sam said, finally.

"And you wouldn't be swayed by the part where a woman discovers the horse," Jake said, reasonably.

"Of course not," Sam said, though the story had her wondering more than ever why Mac had brought her along. Could he think *she* had a special connection with horses? When she got up her courage to ask, though, his eyes were closed. He leaned against the back of the sheltered area, dozing.

Jake noticed at the same time. He stood quietly and motioned her to follow. They walked some distance past the fishermen and around the lake before either of them spoke.

"Is he all right?" Sam asked first.

Jake looked at her, amazed. "Mac? Of course he's all right. Do you mean like crazy or—"

"No," Sam said. She tried to put enough meaning into the word so that she wouldn't have to say exactly what she was thinking. "You know, yesterday, when he was asking if you, like, challenged yourself enough?"

"Oh, I get it. You mean that 'passing over' stuff?" Jake laughed. "Don't take that seriously. Mom told me he was saying that stuff on the day she met him and he was like forty. Not even that old. I think he just does it"—Jake paused and squinted toward the lake—"to remind us that nothing lasts forever and you know, someone *could* die before they get everything done."

Like mom, Sam thought, but she put the notion away for later.

"So why did he bring me, do you think? And what was the point of that story?" Sam asked.

"I'll tell you what I think, but you're not allowed to get mad until I'm finished talking, okay?"

Jake would never make a salesman, Sam decided.

He started off telling her that he was going to make her mad.

"Okay," she said. "Just out of curiosity, I'll wait to bite your head off."

"Thanks." Jake drew a deep breath. "The filly doesn't need a good rider. She needs a good friend."

"And I'm going to be her friend?" Sam asked.

"Hush," Jake said. "I'm not sure I've got it straight. Don't interrupt a minute."

"Don't interrupt, don't get mad . . ." Sam listed, rolling her eyes, but then she closed her lips and waited.

"Mac thinks she might trust you. And if you trust me, it might be sort of like a character reference. Does that make sense?"

"Yeah. I used to think that if Ace could just talk to Blackie for me, he'd know it was okay to trust me, even though he'd been hurt by other people."

"Right," Jake nodded vigorously. "So this is what I think. We start meeting every minute we have time between now and next Friday, to make a plan on how to catch her."

"Next Friday? Jake, we only have two weeks. We can't throw away one of them."

"We won't. We're going to plan. Think about it, Sam. Once we have her, we need to spend every waking moment—cancel that. Every moment, waking or sleeping, with her. You know, that's how warriors did it. They let their war ponies sleep in their tents. And sheikhs in the desert? Their war mares slept in their tents and their kids cuddled up and slept with them. Imagine, hundreds of pounds of potentially dangerous horse, and they let their little kids sleep by those hooves. It's gotta be the way to win."

Sam nodded. Jake was probably right.

"So will you help me?" Jake asked.

Help him. Sam turned the words over in her mind. That didn't exactly mean ride with him, as his partner. How could she weasel it out of him?

"Okay," she said. "Until race day, I guess."

Jake looked as if he'd been kicked in the head. "Why—why just until race day?"

"Well, you know, I'll have to get my own stuff ready."

"Yeah . . . ," Jake said. He stared at her as if she weren't too bright. Then, all at once his expression changed to anger. "But you're riding with me, right?"

"Riding with you . . . ?"

"As my partner," he said in a forced calm, "in the race."

"What makes you so sure?" Sam asked.

"Are you teasing, or what?"

"No, I'm just asking you, what makes you so sure I'll be riding as your partner? Have we talked about it? Have you asked if I think Ace is up to it? Have you wondered for just a second if I made plans to ride with someone else?"

It was quiet for a full minute.

A flock of seagulls passed overhead, checked out the humans below, and prepared to land and see if they'd dropped any food.

"Like who?" Jake shouted suddenly, and the flock gave a few scattered cries, banked away from the shore and flew away.

"Like anybody," Sam yelled back. "Dad or Ryan or Pepper . . ."

"Ride with me, Sam," Jake said, "and you won't have idiot people—like me—thinking you're a less-than-great rider. Especially your dad. I saw the way you flinched when Wyatt told you to be careful."

"Oh, like you've gotten over my accident?"

"I'm trying, but—"

"But, if I fell or something, would you decide the very day before the race that it was just too dangerous for poor little Samantha?"

Ever since she'd come home, Jake had been protective of her. He still felt guilty over her accident years ago, because he'd been with her, because he'd felt responsible.

"I am trying," Jake repeated. He drew himself up to his full height, crossed his arms, and looked down at her.

Sam stared right back. Jake couldn't intimidate her into being his partner.

"You're going to have to come up with something better than that," Sam told him.

Jake took a deep breath and looked at her again. This time he raised one eyebrow and smiled. "Be my partner and I promise we'll win."

Chapter Nine

When Sam arrived home and announced that she and Jake would be riding as partners in Mrs. Allen's Super Bowl of Horsemanship, she thought the hard part was behind her.

She was wrong.

Dad didn't stop what he was doing. He kept using a heavy rasp to smooth something on Tank's hoof.

Ross stood at the big Quarter horse's head, looking as if he'd rather be anywhere else, but Sam couldn't figure out why.

"Dad, did you hear me?" Sam asked. "Jake and I are going to be partners in the race."

Dad lowered·Tank's hoof, gave the horse a shoulder pat, then slowly straightened. He pressed both hands to the small of his back and made a small noise of pain. Then, instead of answering, he glanced at Ross.

"You and Pepper want to finish this up?"

Sam stiffened. Dad was turning his chore over to the cowboys. If that was because he wanted to give her his full attention, she wasn't sure she wanted it.

"Sure," Ross said. He looked pleased to be left out of their discussion.

Dad dusted his hands off on his jeans and motioned for Sam to walk beside him back to the house. She did, but with each step, she tried to interpret Dad's silence.

"I thought you'd be excited," she said after about ten steps.

"That's one way of puttin' it."

Sam looked sideways at him. Dad didn't seem mad, exactly, but he sure wasn't overjoyed.

"We'll be careful," she offered.

"Yeah," Dad said, but that didn't count as permission.

As soon as they walked into the house, Dad called a family meeting.

Sam crossed her arms and pressed her lips together, waiting as everyone stopped what they were doing to assemble at the kitchen table.

"It's not that big a deal," she said softly, but no one paid attention.

Gram folded up the order blank she'd been filling out for a seed catalog.

Dad called up the stairs to Brynna.

"I was ready for a break," Brynna said. "My end-of-winter range condition report has got to get finished, but I was dying for a glass of water."

She got her water and sat at the kitchen table, rubbing her eyes.

"Tell them what you told me," Dad instructed Sam.

Sam took a deep breath. "Jake and I are going to be partners in Mrs. Allen's race."

Gram and Brynna looked as baffled as she felt, but Dad's hands were folded together on the table in one big fist.

Sam filled the silence as best she could.

"I'm thirteen years old. I've been raised to be a cowgirl, right?" she asked.

Dad gave a grudging nod.

"And the entire point of Mrs. Allen having coed teams is that things will be safe," Sam added.

Her English teacher had told the class that three good points was enough to persuade a normal person to believe what you were saying, but Sam decided Dad just might not be normal.

So she added one more.

"I'll be riding Ace. I know him and I know the terrain. He's a good horse and I can depend on him."

Brynna and Gram both looked at Dad.

They're on my side, Sam thought. So why don't they jump in and say something? And then, Gram did.

"Samantha, did it ever occur to you to ask permission, rather than coming home and declaring what you were going to do?"

"Umm . . . no."

"And I wonder if you've decided how you'll pay the entry fee?" Brynna added.

"Don't be looking at me," Dad said, when she did. "If I had a hundred-dollar bill I'd be giving it to the power company."

Sam didn't bury her face in her hands, but that's just what she felt like doing. Not asking permission wasn't a big thing. She could take care of that in a single minute. But why hadn't she remembered the money?

"I was thinking that I could use the money I earned from selling Tinkerbell," Sam said.

After saving the big brown draft horse from slaughter, Sam had sold him to Sterling Stables. But she knew exactly what Brynna would say, and she did.

"That's an exciting idea," Brynna said, "but we agreed that would go into your college fund."

Sam nodded. She'd felt as if she were soaring and reality had deflated her. Her spirits sank lower and lower.

Brynna wasn't done talking, though, and she sounded way too cheery.

"If it's all right with your Gram and Dad, I say we should check out the details of this race. If it's unsafe, you and Jake won't waste time trying to find the money. On the other hand, if it sounds all right and you and Jake somehow strike it rich, you'll be good to go."

Brynna leaned back in her chair and waited.

"I guess that would be okay," Dad said.

Sam sighed. It wasn't the best news in the world, but it was a start.

For the rest of the evening, Gram and Brynna made phone calls to Mrs. Allen and Dr. Scott, the veterinarian.

With their directions, Gram sketched out the course. She and Dad knew every gulch and gully, each cliff and shaley sidehill.

"There's that thorn thicket that'll rip right through those lightweight chinks of yours," Dad said, tapping Gram's map.

All the while, Sam felt Brynna watching her. Her stepmother's elbow was on the table. Her chin rested in her palm and her red braid dangled to one side.

Sam was embarrassed. She rode the area between here, Deerpath Ranch, and War Drum Flats all the time. Just the same, she was willing to keep quiet, if they'd come to the right conclusion.

It looked like that was just what would happen. Then, after they'd discussed the terrain, Dad called Dr. Scott for a description of the obstacle course.

Sam realized Brynna was still watching her, tapping the fingers of one hand on the table. Sam tried not to notice. Instead, she listened intently, trying to decipher Dr. Scott's side of the telephone conversation.

"Balloons and whistles," Dad mused, finally. "That's not so bad. The things to step over and through don't worry me. Ace is one range-smart pony."

Sam was smiling by the time Dad hung up.

"You've got my permission," Dad said, at last.

"And mine," Gram said.

"Mine too," Brynna echoed.

Sam thanked her entire family with hugs. She was happy, enough to smile as she went up the stairs to bed.

By the time she lay in bed, staring up at the plaster ceiling, she was wondering why her family couldn't see that using money from her college fund to pay the entry fee would be an investment.

Sam rolled over and closed her eyes. If she and Jake won the race, she'd have more money than before, even with one small deduction for a new saddle.

On the way to the bus stop the next morning, Dad turned Sam's entire day upside down.

"I gave you my permission," he said.

Sam sucked in a breath. Dad expected her to know he was referring to the race, and she did. Had he been thinking about it all night? That couldn't be good.

"Yeah," she said cautiously.

"And you still have it," he assured her. "But things could go wrong, things you can't control. You're still my baby, Samantha. When you were born, your mom and I vowed to protect your life with our own. Now, I don't expect it to come to that . . ." Dad's hand slashed through the air between them, as if he could cut off the possibility. "It's a simple race. Trudy Allen's takin' every precaution to see it stays safe. Just to be sure, though, Brynna and I are entering, too. I'll be there if you need me."

"Thanks, Dad," she said as she climbed out of the truck. But she didn't mean it. Not really.

Sam walked with her head down, walking on the edge of the road where asphalt met scrubby range grass.

It was no surprise that he and Brynna wanted to ride in the race. They could put the prize money toward replacing the old hay truck that kept belching black smoke and breaking down.

But why didn't he say that?

Why did he have to tell her which horse to ride? Why did he have to watch over her every minute? How could she prove she was capable if he wouldn't let her do anything on her own?

When she looked up, Jen was already at the bus stop. Sam smothered a surprised laugh. Jen's appearance knocked the frustration right out of her head.

Jen wore gray corduroy pants and a pink blouse. Those were normal enough, but her purple cardigan with some kind of multicolored bulges all over it was . . . bizarre.

"Check out my latest purchase," Jen said. She pulled the sweater closed with one hand and made an artistic gesture with the other.

Jen loved to shop at thrift stores and her taste was what Brynna called "original."

"Nice," Sam managed. She couldn't help squinting a bit closer. "Are those pom-pom things . . . ?"

"Easter eggs," Jen said with satisfaction. "Is this cool, or what?"

"Cool," Sam said, but now that Dad had driven away, the silence around them seemed brittle.

A quail's call came from somewhere nearby. And far off, there was a clunk-clang of Dad's tires crossing a cattle guard.

"So," Jen said, "are you riding with Jake?"

"Yeah," Sam said, and her breath rushed out. She didn't add that her Daddy would be watching every move she made. "How about you and Ryan?"

"Yes!" Jen nodded so hard her braids flipped. "Can you believe it?"

"Of course I can. You're a great rider and he wants to win."

Jen waved away Sam's compliments to rush on.

"I tried to talk him out of that whole mustang-tamer idea, but if Jake's doing it . . ." Jen trailed off, eyebrows raised so high that Sam could see them above Jen's glasses.

"He is," she admitted.

"Then there's no question. Ryan will do it, too. But the good part of that is, he wants me to ride Sky Ranger!"

Sky Ranger was a Thoroughbred cross that Linc Slocum rode for endurance work, like chasing mustangs. Once, soon after Sam had arrived, Linc had ridden him after the Phantom. If the stallion and his herd hadn't disappeared into their secret valley, Sky Ranger might have kept pace with them. He was fleet and tireless.

Just then, they heard the chugging sound of the school bus drawing near.

"Do you want to come watch me get on him for the first time after school?" Jen asked.

It wouldn't be a rodeo, Sam knew. If Linc Slocum could ride him, Jen certainly could. Still, Sky Ranger was high-strung and Linc kept him full of grain. It would be worth watching.

"Sure—" Sam had barely pronounced the word when Jen interrupted.

"Ryan could drive you home afterward."

Jen frowned as soon as she said it and Sam wondered if her best friend was mirroring her expression. With Ryan hanging around, watching Jen wouldn't be as much fun.

"I'll have to see," Sam said.

They both looked left. A tiny slice of bright yellow showed as the bus crested the hill. An instant later, its front windows glittered in the spring sun.

Jen and Sam stood quietly, waiting.

"This isn't going to be awkward, is it?" Sam blurted. "I don't want us to be all aggressive about this race."

Jen's smile started slow, then spread until her lips curved in a grin.

"We'll leave that to our partners," Jen said.

The bus stopped. The air brake hissed and the door opened.

The girls hurried down the middle aisle to their usual row and took their usual seat. All around them things looked the same and smelled the same. But Sam felt the change.

Maybe neither of them liked the tension of competition, but they both wanted to win.

Chapter Ten

Sam was entering Mrs. Ely's history class when Jake grabbed her elbow.

"Ow! What?" she asked. It didn't hurt, but he'd surprised her. She'd been gloomily watching Jen walk away toward her own first period class.

"She riding with Slocum?" Jake nodded after Jen.

"I'm not going to be your spy," Sam snapped.

Jake gave her a bland look, waiting. At last Sam sighed. Jake would find out soon, anyway.

"With Ryan," Sam said, though of course that was who Jake had meant. Linc was a cruel and inept rider and Rachel thought horses were smelly and boring. Besides, she was in France.

Jake stood solid amid the students dodging around him and sprinting toward classes. He stared at the place in the hall where Jen had been, though she'd turned a corner and vanished.

"He doesn't go to school," Jake said.

Sam was used to mining Jake's remarks for their meaning and she thought she knew what he meant this time.

"So he's got more time to work with Roman," Sam suggested. She went on after Jake nodded. "But it will all even out, because Jen's riding Sky. He's flighty and it will take her a while to get comfortable with him. I'll be riding Ace. We know each other inside and out. And"— Sam raised her voice when Jake shifted impatiently—"Roman's never been haltered, let alone ridden, but the pinto filly has some experience with a rider."

"All bad," Jake said.

"But she's not going to think you're trying to wrap a snake around her head when you approach with a bridle," Sam said. "And don't forget she was raised by nice people."

"Maryann Pete," Jake said, nodding.

"Until she was a yearling, she was happy around humans," Sam insisted.

As the tardy bell rang, Sam stepped back inside the classroom. She glanced over her shoulder in time to see Mrs. Ely. Blond hair curled and bouncing, she clicked into the classroom's back door on her high heels.

She pointed a finger at Sam and motioned her into class.

Sam knew she'd be counted present and on time,

but Jake would be late.

"Oh, man." He sighed.

"Ask your mom for a pass," Sam whispered.

"I'd have a better chance getting that hundred dollars from her," Jake sounded sour, but sure.

As he started away, he shouted back over his shoulder. "We'll talk after school, okay? And drive the Scout out to Monument Lake."

As he sprinted down the empty hallway, Sam was filled with disbelief. First, he'd assumed she'd be his partner. Now, Jake assumed she'd hang around with him after school.

Was she supposed to just ditch Jen?

"Miss Forster," Mrs. Ely's sarcasm snapped Sam back to history class. "Were you planning on handing in your weekend homework or are you acting as hallway sentry, today?"

Sam let the door slam. Her classmates smiled as she headed for her desk.

"I've got it," Sam said, as she slipped into her seat. At least Rachel was out of the country instead of sitting in the desk behind hers, rolling her eyes.

Sam unzipped her backpack and rummaged through it.

"It's here, really," Sam said as Mrs. Ely tapped her toe in annoyance. "I found it!"

Sam passed the paper forward and hoped it would be that easy to find an excuse to tell Jen.

During their lunch hour, both girls stood outside, munching sandwiches and apples. For months, the weather had been so harsh, they'd had to eat in the cafeteria. Now it was cool and sunny.

They were enjoying the warmth of sun on their cheeks and talking as usual when Jen mentioned she'd received a message in her last class.

"I forgot, I have a dentist appointment," she said with a pout. "I guess riding Sky will have to wait until tomorrow."

"Do it when you get home, Jen. I don't have to be there to watch. We have less than two weeks."

"Yeah, I know. I wouldn't be worried, except for Roman. What do you remember about him?"

"Not that much," Sam said slowly. "He's dark chestnut with a pretty extreme Roman nose and he acts like a stallion."

"I was just thinking—oh, forget it. I'm beginning to sound like you."

"Oh, now I really have to hear it," Sam said. "Spit it out."

"Well, the race runs over the Phantom's territory, right?" Jen asked. "And this is the time of year herd stallions guard their mares against other stallions. They're superjealous, right?"

"Why didn't I think of that?" Sam wondered aloud. "There are bound to be some stallions in the race. What if the Phantom challenges them?"

"I don't think it will happen," Jen said as the bell rang for the end of lunch hour. "The noise and riders would scare off the usual mustang."

As she walked toward Journalism, her last class

of the day, Sam was thinking that she and Jen both knew the Phantom was a very *un*usual mustang. She'd raised him from birth and he'd lived as a domestic horse until the accident that had put her in a coma and set him free.

While Sam lived in San Francisco, recovering, the young stallion had run wild, but he hadn't forgotten her.

He might have been easy to recapture and gentle, if his encounters with people hadn't taught him fear.

The silver mustang's beauty had drawn humans who wanted to capture him. Some, like Linc Slocum, hadn't cared if they'd scared and injured him.

Suddenly a charge of excitement flashed through her. Of course the Phantom hated some humans, but he trusted her as much as a wild thing could.

The situation could be exactly the same for Jake and the filly.

Sam couldn't get her mind off horses. The current events quiz in Journalism didn't do it and neither did typing her story for the next issue of the *Darton Dialogue*.

Her fingers lifted right off the computer keys when an idea struck her.

Saturday night, she'd dreamed of the Phantom. This morning, she'd noticed she'd scratched her wrist. Even in her sleep, she'd been checking her wrist for the lost bracelet woven of the stallion's hair.

What if he'd come to the river Saturday and

Sunday nights, but she'd been sleeping too deeply to wake completely? Could she have half heard him, and woven his call into her dreams?

It was possible.

Sam typed another sentence, then stared into the computer screen. Jen wouldn't get off the bus with her today. She'd be walking home alone. If the Phantom was nearby he might come to her.

"Forster! Take a nap on your own time. I need that story!" Mr. Blair shouted.

Frowning at the screen, as if she was concentrating, Sam waved one hand to let Mr. Blair know she'd heard.

She glanced at the classroom clock. Fifteen minutes until she could leave. Another twenty-five, or so, until the bus dropped her off.

Sam's fingers danced on the keys, faster than ever before. She had to finish this story now. If Mr. Blair kept her in and she missed the bus, she'd miss a chance to see the Phantom.

After class, Jake was waiting outside.

Sam fiddled with her backpack, adjusting it to sit just right. She wasn't sure what to tell him.

"Ready?" he shifted from foot to foot as if she'd been stalling for hours.

"Excuse me," she said, slipping past him. "I'm taking the bus home." She paused, feeling guilty because he looked so surprised. "You know Gram will go nuts if I just take off without asking permission."

It was true, but it wasn't the reason she didn't want to go with him. Somehow, Jake seemed to know.

"Okay," he bit the word short and headed down the hall.

"What if . . ." Sam said, before he got too far.

Jake turned and Sam hurried after him. They were outside now. She could see the bus idling, waiting.

A gust of warm spring wind blew from behind her, sending her red-brown hair into a frenzy around her face.

Frustrated, she pushed it back with both hands, then ordered her brain to come up with something.

"Since we saw the filly in the morning at Monument Lake—"

Sam stopped, filled with disbelief for what she'd nearly said. Jake raised his black eyebrows, but he didn't meet her gaze. In fact, he seemed focused on her hair. Probably so she wouldn't see the disappointment in his eyes.

"Why don't we go tomorrow before school," she blurted.

Say no, say no, say no, she begged silently.

"Good idea." Jake nodded slowly. "Dad won't complain about undone chores, either, since I'm not doin' anything at five A.M. Pick you up then."

Stupid, stupid, stupid. Sam wondered if she was weaving with shock as she started toward the bus.

"Hey, Brat?" Jake called after her.

Sam whirled, hoping no one had heard the baby-
ish nickname.

"What?" she hissed.

Jake used one hand to make a vague smoothing
gesture at his hair. "Do somethin'. You look kinda
like, uh, what's that flower with the petals goin' every
which way? Like a chrysanthemum."

If she hadn't already been so embarrassed her
face hurt from blushing, Sam would have screamed.

With a little planning, she could have picked a
better friend than Jake Ely. A friend who didn't
mock her or force her to get up early.

Civilized human beings didn't get out of bed at
five o'clock in the morning twice in one week, she
thought, as she trudged up the steps, onto the bus.
The rooster didn't crow that early. It was still night!

She found a seat and squinted at her reflection in
the windowpane. She couldn't see much except her
outline, so she smoothed both hands over her hair,
then leaned her forehead against the cold glass.

She could probably catch a catnap now, and store
up sleep. But there was no way she was going to take
a chance of missing a glimpse of the wild horses.

Once the bus had stopped at the junior high
school to pick up a few more students, it rolled out
of Darton. They passed the mall, the scattered gas
stations, mini-marts, and most of the other bus
stops and rolled onto the highway, then Sam began
searching the far hills.

She couldn't see much without binoculars, but

she watched for movement. When the bus stopped at Clara's Diner to let off a few students, Sam sat up straighter. Lost Canyon, Arroyo Azul, and War Drum Flats were east of here and she'd seen the Phantom's herd here before.

There! Sam bounced up in her seat. Below the ridgeline, in a clump of juniper that was starting to green up, she thought something moved. Something.

"Did you see those antelope?" crowed a voice behind her. "My dad says there's enough of 'em to crowd out the nags this year."

Sam twisted and glared over the seat back. If looks could kill, whoever was back there was dead meat.

"The *what*?" she demanded.

Two younger boys shrank away as far as their seat would allow, then stared up at Sam, openmouthed.

"The, uh—" His chin ducked as he swallowed. "I don't know any nicer names for 'em, honest."

"Mustangs," Sam said, carefully. "Wild horses."

"Okay," the boys said, together.

Sam turned around. It would be mean to lecture the boys, since they looked so scared.

She didn't hear another peep from them for several miles. When her stop came up, Sam stood and held the seat in front of her for balance. As the bus slowed, she pulled on her backpack. Two loud whispers came from behind her.

"She got real fierce about those horses."

"Yeah, with all that crazy red hair, she looked like a lion!"

The bus braked, stopped, and Sam stepped out into the aisle. Before she left, she turned and fixed the two boys with the most threatening glare she could manage.

A lion. A chrysanthemum.

As she left the bus, Sam wondered what she really looked like. She didn't want to care.

Why couldn't she live like a horse? A horse didn't give a thought to the way it looked.

As she stepped off the last step of the bus and reached the ground, Sam took in a deep breath of desert air. The next best thing to being a horse was being with them.

The bus pulled away, leaving her alone in wild horse country.

Slow-footed and loose-jointed, Sam started walking for home. If the Phantom was watching, she wanted him to see no threat from her.

She peered at each clutter of boulders and cluster of sagebrush. She studied the eastern hills. From here, she could see the winter-grayed sagebrush was turning green, but she saw no horses.

Every few steps, she thought she heard a faint scuff. She stopped, listened, and looked back. She saw the high desert, beige and gray and white. She heard the fretting of quail, but there were no leaves to rustle and no insects to buzz.

She took three more steps, before she felt a warm, itching sensation between her shoulder blades. Then came a crunch. As she whirled to look again, she saw the horses.

Tiny and far off, the mares were scattered over the hillside like wildflowers. Half-grown colts and fillies moved among them. But they were too far away. The sound couldn't have been them.

Sam cupped a hand on each side of her face, around her eyes, trying to block out the desert's glare.

The horses were eating, moving slowly over the rock-strewn slant, grabbing mouthfuls of short spring grass wherever they spotted it.

She looked higher on the hillside. The Phantom usually kept watch instead of eating, but she didn't see him.

Sam glanced at her watch. It was a silly thing to do. She was going to cross the road and walk toward the hillside whether she had time or not.

A snort, loud and accusing, made her stop.

The snort hadn't carried to her on the wind. It came from behind her. She didn't move, but the horse did.

A hoof struck the alkali flat.

Sam looked down. Her shadow showed black on the white playa, but she wasn't alone. A bigger shadow overlapped hers.

How could he have materialized out of the desert air?

Every single step from the bus stop, she'd watched for him.

He couldn't be there, and yet she knew he was. She could smell his leathery sweet scent. She felt heat radiate from his big body. Her thoughts couldn't have wished him into being, and yet . . .

She studied the shadow again. The horse's outline showed no rider.

Her pulse beat fast and wild. No mustang except the Phantom would have followed her.

"Zanzibar," she whispered.

The low nicker said he knew his secret name. She felt his warm breath through her shirt.

Could she turn and face him? Sam ached to look at the horse close up and see how he'd come through the hard winter. Was he too close? Would he shy and gallop away? It had happened before, but Sam had to risk it.

Moving an inch at a time, she turned her head right, letting it lead her shoulder and her foot. Measuring each movement by the sound of the stallion's breathing, she managed to turn three-quarters of the way toward him before he backed off.

Sam froze. She swallowed. In the silence she thought she could hear the mares' teeth grinding on the hillside and then, in a flurry of pounding hooves, the Phantom was right in front of her.

"Hey, boy," Sam whispered. She barely got the words out through her smile.

He backed a few steps, snatched a quick glance at his mares, then huffed through his nostrils and tossed his thick forelock from merry eyes.

Sam looked him over quickly.

No one would mistake the stallion for a barn-sheltered show horse. Most of his hair was white and clumpy. From his fuzzy ears to his shaggy fetlocks, he looked like a mustang who'd kept himself warm with no help from humans.

"Still got on your winter woollies, don't you, boy?"

At the sound of her voice, the stallion shivered. His eyes opened wider and he leaned forward with an avid look just before he closed the space between them.

Sam's sigh came out shaky and satisfied. She raised her hand to touch his neck. When he didn't shy away or bowl her over, she stroked his shoulder. Then, holding her breath, she let her fingers skim over his barrel.

She couldn't see his ribs, but she felt them. Beneath his winter coat, in patches, she saw the gleam of fine silver hair.

All at once, the Phantom lurched forward. Sam side stepped.

"What's wrong, boy?" Sam's heart thundered as the stallion fell to his knees. She remembered that awful night in the rodeo arena when the stallion had been drugged and dizzy. This didn't look the same.

Sam scanned the terrain around her. For one weird moment, she wondered if he'd been darted with a tranquilizer gun. He'd gone down that fast. But he wasn't unconscious.

Groaning, he slammed to his side on the desert floor.

"I get it," Sam chattered, jumping out of the way of the stallion's thrashing legs. "Scare me to death, why don't you?"

Moaning so loudly that his mares must wonder

what she'd done to their king, the Phantom rolled. He was rubbing off his winter coat, scratching his back on the bone-white alkali flat, and loving every second of it.

Sam laughed. The most magnificent animal in the world, squirming like a puppy.

For those few seconds, he was totally vulnerable to attack from another stallion. He trusted her to stand guard.

His vacation only lasted a few moments. He lurched to his feet, shook off a snowstorm of loose hair, then launched himself away. His back hooves scraped, dug in, and Sam blinked against the dirt peppering her face.

The stallion burst into a gallop. Stretching and turning, he ascended the zigzag path up the hillside to his mares.

They saw him coming, slinging his head in a herding motion. They ran.

The mares vanished over the crest of the hill. Sam waited for the Phantom to run into sight. He should be just behind them. She waited, waited, and finally let out the breath she'd been holding. He must have taken a shortcut she couldn't see from here.

No wonder the horse seemed magical.

She looked at her watch. She couldn't believe she'd looked at it just three minutes ago.

Chapter Eleven

$\mathcal{A}$t five o'clock in the morning, Sam stood in the kitchen, dressed and ready to go.

Luckily she'd left her backpack by the front door last night before she went to bed, because she wouldn't have been able to get everything together now.

She barely had the energy to stare out the window, waiting for the Scout's headlights to pierce the darkness.

She'd almost ignored her alarm. Her eyes had refused to open and her sleepy body had nearly convinced her mind it was the weekend, not Tuesday. Her mind had won the battle. She'd tumbled out of bed and made it down here. Now Jake was late.

When he finally pulled up and she opened the

passenger's side door, the aroma of hot chocolate floated to her.

"Oh, *yes*." How could she scold Jake for being late, when he'd taken extra minutes for this? She took the mug, wrapped her cold hands around it, and inhaled.

They sat quietly until the Scout jounced off the highway, taking the road toward Monument Lake.

"Yesterday, did you see anybody looking at the bumper sticker?" Jake asked.

It took Sam a few seconds to realize Jake was referring to the Columbus sticker on the Scout's back bumper. And she knew why. Most people would probably think it was funny, but it seemed to proclaim the driver as Indian.

"No," Sam said, but didn't point out that she'd only been in the parking lot for a few minutes before and after school.

"I don't want anyone to know about the initiation stuff."

"Okay," Sam said.

"I'm not, like, embarrassed to be Indian. Everyone knows, after all. But I don't want to talk about it. They'll think I have to climb a mountain and catch an eagle or something."

Quick as a light switch snapping on, then off, Sam saw a mental image of the red-tailed hawk's feather sitting in her desk drawer at home.

"That's fine," Sam said. "I'm not going to make a big deal of it."

She'd wanted that feather for Jake, but now she wasn't sure he'd appreciate it.

"Grandfather's got my brothers all ticked off about Slocum's buffalo," Jake said with a sigh. "He says the Indian, wild horse, and buffalo all lost their freedom at the same time. He's making a big symbol out of it."

Jake glanced over for Sam's reaction. She didn't move a muscle. She wasn't sure exactly what he meant about symbolism. That sounded like something her English teacher would say.

But she did know that in history, Mrs. Ely had told of trains carrying tourists west in the early 1800s. As the visitors steamed along, they shot buffalo by the thousands. For fun.

Mrs. Ely had described a curly brown carpet of dead buffalo alongside the train tracks. The wounded buffalo were left to suffer, die, and decay. The tribes who'd depended on them for food and clothing had suffered, too.

But Sam didn't say anything. Jake had always been touchy about his heritage. Unless he asked her a direct question, she'd keep quiet.

"Grandfather's going to give us the entry fee."

"What?" she yelped. That news demanded a reaction.

"He says it's an early graduation present."

"I guess," Sam said. Jake was only a junior. "Way early. Is he that sure you'll graduate?" she teased.

"Yeah," Jake said. In the dark car, his smile shone white. Jake got all A's and B's, and he was a track star. Most ranch boys with his heavy responsibilities couldn't claim so much. He had a right to look proud.

Jake turned off the car key and coasted into the same lookout his grandfather had used on Sunday. Inch by silent inch, he pulled on the parking brake.

Shivering against the morning cold, they followed the path down to the shore. Gulls were gliding above the lake and bobbing on its surface, but they took little notice of the humans. Jake and Sam found the little cave they'd sheltered in before, sat down, and waited.

Sam wiggled the fingers of each hand up the cuff of the opposite coat sleeve. It was relatively cozy, here, but for a minute, she wished that Jen were sitting beside her instead of Jake.

To Jen, she might confide her secret about Dad and Brynna riding in the race. They'd been planning it last night, all giddy and excited, as if it weren't an insult.

Dad planned to ride Nike. Brynna couldn't decide between Jeepers-Creepers and Penny, the blind mustang she rode to get from place to place at Willow Springs.

Neither of them had apologized for riding herd on her.

She must have made some sound of disgust, because Jake frowned at her.

Jake was yawning when Sam heard the horses.

"Here they come," she whispered.

A smooth clinking sound, as if someone stirred a vat of marbles with a bare hand, made one of the gulls rise off the lake, screeching.

The tribal herd moved through the mist.

This time Sam saw the bay stallion lunge ahead of the mares. He studied his surroundings before cautiously lowering his head to drink. He must be their leader. She'd seen the Phantom do exactly the same thing, making sure all was safe before he allowed his band to drink and took his place on a rise to watch over them.

Jaunty and sure, the paint filly trotted ahead of the rest of the herd. Surrounded by the other horses' shades of brown, her black-and-white markings were dramatic.

Wind cleared the mist and the spring morning was bright enough to see the night black that crowned the filly's ears, covered her eyes, then curved to make a dark throat latch. A broad white blaze showed on her slender face. From her throat, the shining black formed a shield across her chest, swooped along her belly, and covered her to all four knees. Both her mane and tail were variegated with black and white.

Sitting shoulder to shoulder and leaning forward with Jake, Sam felt him shake his head in disbelief.

Elegant yet strong, with spark in her eyes and

energy in her stride, the filly was everything a horse should be. And Mac Ely had said she was Jake's for the taking.

"We're going to start talking, quietly, so they know we're here," Jake said.

The filly skittered into the water at the sound of Jake's voice. The broad-chested sorrel snorted and stopped.

"Okay," Sam said.

The dun broke from the herd and actually walked a few steps closer.

"At least half are domesticated. See the rub marks on their noses?"

"From halters."

"And the dun. Look at his legs."

Sam looked, but it took her a few minutes to see what Jake was talking about. The rust-colored barring on the horse's legs almost hid the marks on his front pasterns.

"Hobbles?" Sam asked. "You think someone kept him hobbled at night instead of penning him?"

Jake shrugged and stood up. Sam did, as well.

Most of the horses shied. They were still half a football field away, but they paid close attention to the humans.

The bay shambled down from his lookout to stand between the herd and the humans. His nostrils flared. Open, closed, open.

Sam realized she was breathing with him. Wet

rocks, sage, a mossy green scent. He must have sucked all those smells in with their human ones.

"They're not running," Jake sounded triumphant. He rummaged in his pocket, then said, "Let's walk a little closer."

Even Sam could smell the sweet grain he'd taken from his pocket.

The dun and sorrel nickered in unison. When the other horses, all but the pinto, took a few steps forward, the dun's curiosity and hunger overcame shyness.

Holding his head high, placing his hooves with caution that could turn to an about-face, he came so close, his extended nose could reach Jake's hand.

Whuffling loudly, he took the grain, then tossed his head. Heeding that signal, the other horses crowded forward.

Jake dug into his other pocket. There couldn't be much grain in two jeans pockets. He was just keeping their interest. He had it. Only the pinto stayed by the lake.

Jake scraped the last sticky grains from his left pocket and moved toward the filly.

Her head went higher, then turned to face him. Her dark eyes glinted, sizing him up. Though he moved toward her with horses all around him, as if he were part of the herd, the filly wasn't fooled.

"What are you doing?" Sam asked, but Jake pretended he was already out of earshot.

With the spell broken, Sam looked at her watch. It was six thirty. They still had plenty of time to make it to school, but she'd been hoping they could stop at Clara's for a muffin or something.

Jake must have crossed some invisible boundary, because the filly lifted her knees in a stately walk away from him. When he kept coming, she broke into a lope and the other horses joined her.

"Careful!" Sam shouted.

Why didn't Jake stop? He knew horses. He knew it was idiocy to try to run with a herd. When the bay stallion surged up from behind and clipped his shoulder, it was a warning.

Jake ignored it.

The band had a quarter-mile lead on Jake now, but he kept following.

"You are *such* an idiot," Sam muttered.

He'd left her here to go chasing after them. And the worst part was, Jake could run for a long time. His training runs were seven to ten miles, every day.

This made absolutely no sense. It was completely opposite to what he'd advise anyone else to do.

Sam paced along the shoreline. Hands in fists, teeth set against each other, she took ten strides to the left, then turned. Stomach growling, she counted ten steps back the other way, then stared.

The horses had vanished over a rise at the far end of the lake. Where was Jake?

She looked at her watch again. Seven o'clock.

Classes started at eight. They could still make it.

Low-hanging clouds had turned the yellow sunlight watery. The air had turned colder, and the pale triangular rock in the middle of the lake blocked much of her view.

At eight minutes after seven, Sam looked up at the Scout. If she could drive, she'd leave Jake here.

That would be justice. How hard could it be, anyway? There was nothing out here to hit. It wasn't like she'd drive into the lake.

Sam sprinted up the path and stood panting next to the car. She wouldn't steal his grandfather's car. Just drive it away a little bit to scare him. It would serve him right.

She peered through the driver's side window. He hadn't left the keys in the ignition. Maybe they were under the seat.

She stared a minute. There were *three* pedals on the floor of the car. What could they all be for?

"D-don't," Jake's breathless words carried from the lake shore. "Don't e . . ."

His footsteps covered his words, but Sam didn't back off. Leaning against the driver's side of the car, arms crossed, she sneaked a look at her watch.

Seven fifteen. They'd be cutting it awfully close.

Jake's black hair stuck to his forehead and neck. He wiped his forearm across his brow.

"Don't even think about it," he managed at last.

When she didn't move, he opened the car door

anyway, reached into the door pocket, and retrieved a plain silver ring holding two keys. Why hadn't she thought to look there?

Jake put his hands on his hips and drew a deep breath, then expelled it loudly.

"I know how we're going to catch her," he said.

"That's great," Sam sputtered. "You had some brainstorm while I was up here freezing."

"Let's go," Jake said. He took another deep breath and smiled.

She'd read about runners experiencing a relaxed sense of well-being. She'd never expected it to be so annoying.

"Jake, I suppose you're not going to give me any explanation of why you did such an immature, dangerous . . ."

Jake sighed. "Sam, we can talk about this later." Jake shook his head in a paternal way. "But can you please just get in the car? You're about to make us late."

Chapter Twelve

"Here's what we're going to do," Jake began.

"I'm not listening to a word you say until I eat," Sam said.

Jake stared at her with openmouthed surprise. "This isn't meals on wheels, y'know." Then he turned back to the windshield, jaw set. "I don't have anything."

Jake was not a good liar.

Sam couldn't believe he'd even tried.

"Do you want me to faint in your mom's class? 'Cause that's what's going to happen if I don't get something to eat."

Sam stared out her window. She listened as Jake made an impatient sound, and she smiled. It probably wouldn't be necessary to moan.

"Unzip the front pocket of my backpack," he said, finally. "I've got dried fruit and a couple energy bars."

By the time he finished his sentence, Sam was already hanging over the backseat, retrieving his pack.

"Leave me something, okay? I'm the one who did the running. I need to refuel."

"Yeah," Sam said, chewing. "What was that all about?"

"We're going to run her down."

Sam stopped crumpling the foil from the energy bar. "Run her down?"

Jake nodded. "I've read how. It's the least violent way to catch her. A lot like the shadowing we do in the corral. As long as she runs, I'll go after her. When she stops, I stop. If she comes toward me, I turn my back and ignore her. Eventually she walks up to me and we halter her."

Sam could picture it. At the lake, the filly had been cautious around them, but not terrified.

Sam could believe the pinto's year with Maryann Pete and her grandchildren would overshadow the fearful memory of Shan Stonerow. But Jake had forgotten to figure in one thing.

"Witch isn't going to like it," Sam warned.

The big black Quarter horse had an attitude problem, especially with other mares.

"Witch isn't going to be with us," Jake said. "Just Ace."

The announcement surprised her, but instantly she knew the two horses would get along. Still,

Jake could have said *please*.

"You want to borrow Ace?" she asked.

"No, I'm going to run after the filly on foot."

"What? You must be joking!"

Jake ignored her astonishment and kept talking.

"You're going to hang back on Ace and carry water so I don't die while I'm doing it."

Sam stared at Jake. He was driving as if he hadn't said something insane. And, since she'd heard you were supposed to act calm around crazy people, she tried.

"I know you've been in training for track season and I know you're a good runner, but Jake, she could run you a hundred miles over this range!"

"She could, but I'm hoping she won't."

Sam stared at Jake. This was totally unlike him. *She* was the queen of blind faith. Jake usually calculated his actions so the result was a sure thing.

"Grandfather's really getting into this. He's been telling me how running is part of the spiritual side of a lot of tribes. He says if you're in reasonable shape, you can get in the zone and do it."

Sam swallowed hard. "It sounds cool," she admitted, "but isn't it a little risky?"

"If I feel awful, I'll stop," Jake said.

But she couldn't just let him brush off her concern.

"What if you exhaust yourself running and you're too tired to handle the filly's training? And then there's the race, of course. Are you sure you can do it?"

"No." Jake's broad smile contradicted the word,

until he went on. "And that's the point, according to Grandfather. I've got to attempt something I only *hope* I can do."

They were in sight of school, with eight minutes before the first bell rang, when Jake asked, "Do you think Wyatt will let you camp out by Monument Lake? Grandfather will be with us. If we tame the filly out on the range, train her without fences, maybe her bad memories won't return."

"If your grandfather asks Dad, maybe . . . ," Sam said. She knew Jake was a wizard with horses, but this manhood thing was sounding more and more far-fetched. She counted the days they'd have.

Seven?

She counted again, using her fingers this time. Saturday, Sunday, Monday, Tuesday, Wednesday, Thursday, Friday. The race was the following Saturday. Even though spring vacation would help, at best they'd only have seven full days with the filly.

She'd seen a TV special about professional horse trainers who could tame wild horses in a few days. Even they admitted the horses remained unpredictable for months. And Jake, for all his skill, was just a kid.

"Seven days isn't very long," she said, as Jake parked the Scout and they joined the mob of students hustling toward class.

"No, but I'm going to convince our parents that we should leave right from school on Thursday, and since Friday is a minimum day for everyone except sophomores . . ."

Sam's mind spun as she pulled on her backpack.

Jake was right. Sophomores had some sort of statewide test on Friday. Classes would be only thirty minutes long, so the school day would end early. Everyone, except the poor sophomores, would be dismissed at noon.

She was a freshman and Jake was a junior.

Jake gave her a brotherly slap on the back that made her stagger. "We'll have eight and a half days, Brat. Piece of cake!"

The rest of the week passed like a jumbled dream.

Dad, Brynna, and Gram not only agreed to Jake's plan, Brynna started assembling camping supplies and Gram began cooking food that would be easy to reheat over a camp stove. That was the good news.

At school, things weren't so easy. Every one of Sam's teachers promised a spring vacation without homework, but major assignments were due Thursday in every class except P.E. and Journalism.

On Wednesday morning she let Jake go see the pinto alone, while she slept in for another hour. She'd missed talking with Jen at the bus stop, yesterday.

They both felt like it was a reunion. Jen chattered about plans for the Super Bowl of Horsemanship. Ryan had offered to pay the entry fee.

Sam wasn't surprised, until Jen explained that if they won, Ryan wanted to return half the prize money to Mrs. Allen.

"And he'll give half to me," Jen said, with a sappy

smile, "for all my hard work. I bet no one else in the race will be so generous."

Angry heat flashed over Sam. Was it a best friend's job to point out Jen's silly, lovey-dovey expression and her blind approval of anything Ryan did?

Even though she wanted to shake Jen and shout, *Sure, Ryan can afford to be generous. His daddy's a millionaire!*, she didn't do it.

That was probably why, when Jen mentioned that Ryan was having trouble working with Roman, Sam shivered with guilty satisfaction.

That afternoon, when Dad and Pepper rode in muddy and grumpy from clearing irrigation ditches, Sam decided to give Dad one more example of her maturity. When she offered to clean up Tank, Dad gave her a grateful grin.

She worked alongside Pepper, the seventeen-year-old cowboy from Idaho, and found she didn't mind the work. Pepper was tired, but not as disgruntled as Dad, and he wanted to talk.

As they tied Tank and Strawberry to the hitching rail, he confided they'd seen the Phantom.

"You did? Where?"

"Kinda by Lost Canyon," Pepper said, stripping the saddle from Strawberry's roan back. "That wasn't the interestin' part, though."

Sam watched Pepper shake the saddle blanket coated with sweat and loose hair. She gave him a few seconds, knowing she wouldn't have to pry the story out of him.

"He was battlin' another stallion who, I guess, got a little too friendly with the gray's mares."

Instantly, Sam thought of Moon. The Phantom's night-black son had challenged him before. She hoped he wasn't at it again.

"They were kickin' and squealin'," Pepper went on, "and your horse was usin' his teeth so much, he 'bout peeled that sorrel like a potato."

Sorrel. It wasn't Moon, then. Still, Sam cringed. Of course she wanted the Phantom to win every fight, but bites could get infected and she didn't want any mustang to die.

By the time they'd finished grooming both horses, Brynna was home and it was almost dinnertime. Walking to the house, Sam was trying to remember everything she had to do before bedtime.

Homework, of course, and pack for her camping trip. Since she and Jake would leave right after school tomorrow, he was coming by tonight to pick up her gear and stash it in the Scout.

When she got inside, Gram had just finished talking with Mrs. Allen and she was reporting on the conversation to Brynna.

"Well, Trudy's given in to our rich neighbor," Gram began in frustration. She stopped talking, looking a little guilty as soon as she saw Sam.

But then Dad came into the kitchen. He'd already washed up and changed to a fresh shirt for dinner. Sam could smell the pine tar soap he always used.

"How'd she do that?" he asked.

"For a substantial donation, she agreed to let Linc 'display' his bison herd at the start of the race."

"We'll have more *loco* horses than they know what to do with," Dad said.

Sam agreed, and she didn't much like the idea of being *on* one of them. Still, she was curious.

"I'd like to see them," Sam admitted.

"So would I," Brynna said. "But I'd feel better if he had the faintest idea of what he planned to do with them."

"It sounded like he wanted to have hunters pay to shoot them," Gram said.

"If so," Dad said, "he'd better keep 'em penned on his own property. Come hunting season you always hear of dudes shooting a heifer, thinkin' she's a buck. Can't imagine it's any different with buffalo hunters."

They were clearing the dinner dishes when Jake and his grandfather arrived. They loaded her camping gear in the cargo area of the Scout. Gram and Mac still stood outside talking while Sam took Jake inside for dessert.

As soon as he saw Brynna, Jake squared his shoulders and stopped.

"Hello, Jake," Brynna said.

"I had a question," he said. "If . . . well . . . if I run this filly onto public lands, and she mixes in with the wild horses, what happens?"

Sam listened intently. Jake hadn't mentioned his concern over this before.

"Nothing until there was a gather. *If* there was a

gather and she was brought in and *if* there was some identification on her, say, a brand, we'd trace her back to you. Then, you could either claim her and pay the trespass fees for grazing her on public lands for free, or you could give her up to us and we'd try to find her another home."

"There's gotta be some crossover with tribal lands bordering public lands."

"There is," Brynna admitted. "We know some horses wander back and forth and most aren't branded. We wouldn't know they weren't wild unless someone came forward, claimed them, and paid the trespass fees."

Jake looked as if he had another question, but just then his grandfather poked his head inside.

He gave friendly waves to all the Forsters, then looked at Jake and jerked his head toward the car.

"Jacob, let's go. Your mother made me promise to hurry. You'll be sleeping on the ground tomorrow and she wants you to get a good night's sleep tonight."

Without a word of protest, Jake went. Sam was sure she'd never heard him called *Jacob* before. It sounded strangely grown-up, and she wondered if that was why Mac Ely had used it.

Sam got to bed on time, but her sleep was plagued with nightmares.

Just before dawn, she dreamed of a maze. At first she thought she was in one of the ravines branching off the main part of Lost Canyon or Arroyo Azul.

Then she thought she was inside a video game. At last she realized it was a carnival ride, one of those cars with a seat belt and steering wheel, but no matter which way you turned, you really had no choice.

In her dream, it was dark and she rode alone, ears hurting from the blatting sound that warned her of each new danger. First, a mannequin of Jake popped up in her path, blowing a police whistle. Blatt! The car jerked right and there was the Phantom, head snapping forward like a striking snake.

Her dream hands steered frantically away and she barely missed a model of Ryan, arms crossed as he gave a mocking laugh that was instantly drowned by another blatt.

The car ratcheted up a long hill, past Jen on a rearing Sky Ranger with flashing red eyes. At the top of the hill, a big brown buffalo rocked like a hobby-horse. Lightning bolts zigzagged from its nostrils. And just when she thought the nightmare had ended, she rounded one last corner and the car plunged down into darkness. At the bottom, Linc Slocum cackled and took aim at her. Not with a gun. What was it? She tried to put on a brake, but there were too many pedals on the floor of the car. She kept plummeting down, and just before impact, Linc Slocum stopped her by throwing a high-heeled Western boot.

Chapter Thirteen

"You talked in your sleep a lot last night," Brynna said as she drove Sam to the bus stop the next morning.

"I bet I did," Sam said. "I had a crazy dream. You and Dad weren't in it, but you might have been the only ones."

"Are you putting too much pressure on yourself to win this race?"

"Not yet," Sam said. "I haven't even done anything to prepare for it, except check out Jake's horse."

"But it means a lot to you," Brynna said in a leading voice.

Sam looked down at her left wrist. She circled it with her fingers, wishing she'd found her horsehair bracelet. She kept looking down, afraid her face would give her away. She wasn't about to tell Brynna she hoped this race would show Dad she was nearly grown.

"It doesn't mean that much to me," Sam said, once she thought she could trust her face not to give her away. "But Jake really wants the money for his truck fund."

Brynna looked skeptical, but she didn't press for a different answer.

"According to Mac, you'll be camping out near Monument Lake from tonight until at least Sunday. And he's coming by about eleven to pick up Ace and trailer him out there with you."

"Yeah," Sam said. "Ace gets to go to school."

Jake hated the idea. He wanted to keep the entire project quiet. Now, not only was his grandfather, known as a shaman, coming to school with his rust-wrecked Scout and its radical bumper sticker; he would be dragging a horse trailer and horse.

So much for slipping out unnoticed, Sam thought.

"Your Dad will be out to check on you," Brynna said. "He's already talking about bringing you home for a shower . . ."

"We'll be right next to a lake, you know," Sam pointed out.

"Yes, and you know how he is." Brynna kissed Sam on the cheek at the bus stop.

"You be careful, honey," she said, wrapping her in a hug. "See you in a couple days."

By noon, Sam was climbing into the backseat of the old Scout. It smelled of French fries and a fast-food paper bag was waiting on the backseat for her.

"Hello, Samantha," Mac Ely said. "Your horse has been very cooperative. I hope you don't mind a bumpy ride."

"I'll be fine, Mr. Ely," she said, fastening her seat belt, then turning to look through the back window at what she could see of Ace.

"Looks like the circus came to town," Jake muttered.

Sam turned back to see Jake staring straight ahead through the windshield, even when other students pointed and waved.

She did feel a little sorry for him. Jake was a private sort of guy. The only thing he did to draw attention to himself was his running.

She decided this was as good a time as any to give him the little present she'd brought. She unzipped the front pouch on her backpack and withdrew the red-brown hawk's feather she'd been saving for him.

"Here," Sam said. "For luck."

Jake took it, stroked his fingers down the plume, and mumbled a quiet thanks.

"It'll look good in the filly's mane when you ride her in the race," Sam said. "Oh, and about all of them . . ." She gestured at a few kids who were staring at the truck and trailer. "They'll all have forgotten by the end of spring break."

"No, they won't," Mac corrected her. "They'll be

saying, 'Hey, that kid with the weird grandfather? He and his friend won the Super Bowl of Horsemanship!'"

Jake couldn't stifle a faint smile, but it vanished when the Scout's back end scraped and screeched in the school's steep driveway, and its front end pointed up, as if it were about to lift off.

Sam was putting one hand on the door for balance as the Scout bumped out of the lot, toward the freeway, and almost missed seeing Ryan Slocum.

But he saw them.

Driving the baby-blue Mercedes-Benz, he swooped into the school lot, probably to pick up Jen.

As Ryan spotted Jake in the front seat, he frowned, then gave his horn a dignified beep and waved.

"Perfect, just perfect," Jake muttered.

And they were on their way.

Sam loved the high desert, but today, when she was in a hurry to get out of the backseat, away from the smell of the fast food she'd just pounded down, it seemed too much the same.

After miles of sand dotted by green sage and piñon, the sudden appearance of Monument Lake as they topped the rise was a shock.

Both times she'd been here recently, the lake had been veiled with mist. Today, it was as she remembered: a turquoise gem set between chalky pink-and-gray mountains.

The "monument" in the middle was a tufa formation, made of some kind of alkaline chemicals, but it

looked like a giant altar built by an ancient civiliza-
tion. It was alive with movement, covered with gulls.

There was no sign of the tribal herd.

"I wonder where the horses hide out during the
day," Sam said.

"Oh, they're mostly penned," Mac said, nodding.
"Shan Stonerow took them in."

Sam gasped and Jake turned slowly to stare at his
grandfather.

"The pinto's out there, still," Mac added. "I asked
him to leave her for now."

"She'll be lonely and easier to catch," Jake
mused, but he didn't sound grateful. "You didn't have
to make it simple for me."

Mac Ely burst into a laugh and his "just you wait"
expression took in Sam as well.

"Oh, Jacob," Mac said. "While this filly is running you over fifty acres of desert, you'll have plenty
of time to remember those words."

"There's some stuff I didn't tell you," Jake admitted as they climbed out of the Scout.

A camp surrounded by cottonwood trees was
already set up. The tent stood next to stacked firewood, and Chocolate Chip, the Quarter horse
brother of Witch, nickered a greeting.

"I guess so," Sam said. She unlatched the trailer
doors and backed Ace out to join Chip.

Chip dwarfed the mustang. He was only about
two hands taller, but he was muscular and heavy-

boned. His conformation was identical to Witch's, and he was just as fast. Only his dark chocolate coat and mild temperament set the siblings apart.

As Ace and Chip touched noses, Sam remembered her only ride on Chip.

Queen, the red dun who'd been the Phantom's lead mare, had escaped. Sam had ridden after her at a full gallop, on Chip. Suddenly, she didn't wonder why Chip was here.

"You gave up the idea of running her down," Sam said. She kept all reaction from her tone, but she was glad Jake had come to his senses. Then she found out he hadn't.

"Not exactly, but we'll talk while we ride. Wait here. I'll be back."

Jake ducked into the tent to change, without giving Sam a chance to reply.

Maybe it was because she'd been bumped around in the backseat with a belly full of fast food that Sam decided to tell Jake to quit giving her orders.

When he came out of the tent wearing faded green sweatpants and a green-and-gold Darton High sweatshirt with the sleeves hacked off, she was ready for him.

"Jake, I want to do this," she snapped, "but if you don't stop bossing me around, we're going to have a fight. I don't mind you taking the lead, but you just keep assuming stuff. That I'd be your partner and bring Ace along, for a start. And when you changed the plan," she paused, gesturing to take in the camp and horse, "you didn't tell me. Stop doing that."

As Jake recovered from the ambush, Sam sneaked a quick glance at Mac. He busied himself with arranging wood in the stone fire ring, though it wouldn't be dark and cold for hours.

"Okay," Jake said grudgingly. "But I don't know why you can't just go along . . ."

Sam's hands perched on her hips.

"You're not getting this, are you?" she demanded.

"Forget I said that." Jake moved his hands as if erasing his words. "But we need to find that filly and start shadowing her now. This is day one of our eight and a half. From this time on, every minute counts."

Riding double was another thing Jake hadn't mentioned.

"How long do you expect me to do this?" Sam asked.

Sam sat in the actual seat of the exercise saddle. Smaller than a Western saddle, it changed her position and balance. Not only that, but saddlebags were attached to the front of the saddle because Jake sat behind the cantle, where saddlebags would usually go, so that he could dismount in a hurry.

"I'm guessing less than twenty-four hours," Jake said.

"*Twenty-four*—"

"I'll get off to run every time we get close to her," Jake assured Sam. "So you'll have the saddle to yourself."

"I guess that's all right," Sam said. "I can work the

kinks out of my neck when we get back to camp for dinner."

"Well, no," Jake said. "We're not stopping for dinner."

Sam looked at the bulging saddlebags. Dinner must be inside. She wished she'd been more appreciative of her last hot meal, even if it had been a skinny cheeseburger and pale fries.

Sitting behind her as they rode away from camp, Jake still felt tense, as if there was more to tell.

"What else?" she demanded.

Against her spine, Sam felt Jake's chest rise as if he had to draw a deep breath for this next part.

"We won't stop to sleep, either."

Sam wanted to jerk Chip to a stop so sudden, he'd tuck his haunches under and Jake would slide off, onto the ground. But that would be mean. Chip had a tender mouth and was used to being ridden on a loose rein.

Just then, Chip's entire body tensed. He'd spotted the filly.

Her stark black-and-white coat stood out against the stand of juniper where she'd sought shade from the midday sunshine. She stood tall, head turned their way with ears pricked forward.

"I see her," Jake muttered. "Let's go."

Sam sent Chip forward. Instinctively, he knew what they were doing. He shook his head against the reins, fighting to break into his breed's lightning-fast sprint for a quarter mile.

"We had this talk before," Sam told Chip. "I'm the boss and I want you to save it."

Chip settled into a smooth, ground-eating lope.

"'Bout time," Jake complained, but then they both watched the filly.

Understanding this had turned into pursuit, she ran, dodging clumps of sagebrush and boulders, jumping a dry riverbed.

"Just keep her in sight," Jake said.

"That's what I'm doing," Sam told him.

After thirty minutes, the filly showed no sign of slowing.

Jake had instinctively leaned forward into Chip's lope, and Sam was sick of it.

"You're crowding me," she complained.

"Sorry." Jake drew back, sounding embarrassed.

"It's okay," she told him.

A dark rise of earth littered with granite boulders showed just ahead. As the filly scaled it, they could hear her grunts.

Was she finally tiring? Sam urged Chip on faster. Jake's plan was to get within a quarter mile, a horse's natural flight distance, then dismount and pursue her on foot for as long as he could.

In two strong surges, Chip passed over deer trails twining through the dust. He was atop the mound and Sam felt one of Jake's running shoes graze her boot as he got ready to dismount.

The top of the mound was level and Chip came almost to a dead stop. Sam's heels flared away in the stirrup irons, ready to give Chip a boot, but the filly was gone.

Thick with juniper, the other side of the mound descended back to level range that was greener than the territory they'd just covered, but nothing moved.

Chip tugged on the reins. His chocolate ears tipped forward. His hooves danced lightly in indecision. He sniffed and his head swung from side to side, searching.

Sam fanned herself with her Stetson. When had the temperature soared?

"It's not your fault," Sam said, rubbing Chip's wet neck. "We lost her."

A gull coasted overhead. His cry sounded a lot like laughter.

Sweat dripped into Sam's eyes and the small of her back was itchy. It had been chilly when they'd started this run, but now she wanted to shuck off her jacket and throw it on the desert floor.

Sam heard the wind in the gull's feathers as his wings tilted his body right, then left, chuckling as he watched the stupid humans.

She was about to dismount and grab a rock to scare him away, when she felt Jake hop off Chip.

He stood next to her stirrup just long enough to tighten the thong holding his black hair.

"We didn't lose her," he whispered, "She's hiding. Right there."

Chapter Fourteen

Chip trembled, leaning forward to stare in the direction Jake pointed.

Darn, this was just like tracking with Jake. He saw things that were invisible to normal humans.

Placing each footstep precisely, Jake started down. Brush grabbed at his sweatpants, but he moved with a quick and soundless stealth.

Chip tugged at the bit, wanting to follow. Sam kept her reins snug. When Jake did flush the filly from hiding—and she knew he would—Chip couldn't be stampeding over them.

The clink of Chip's bit must have told the filly she was no longer safe.

Black-and-white hide glinted as the filly broke cover and ran. Jake slipped, skidded after her, then regained his feet and settled into his stride.

Now what?

Jake's secret plan hadn't included directions for this. Sam looked at her watch.

They had plenty of daylight left, but the filly's short rest had revitalized her. She ran full out, raising a rooster tail of dust until she passed a row of black sawtooth rocks sticking up from the desert floor.

When the filly stopped to look back, Sam recognized her strategy.

Prey animals survived by getting out of reach first, then turning to see what was after them.

Jake stopped, too, showing the filly he'd only chase if she ran.

The filly wasn't frightened by him, but she didn't understand, either. Jake wasn't acting like any human she'd encountered before.

She made a prancing path among rocks and gave her mane a playful toss.

It's been a lonely, boring day without the others, she seemed to say, *so come on and chase me.*

She bolted, but Jake didn't rush after her. He kept his stride smooth. Once he'd reached the saw-tooth rocks, Sam let Chip go on.

The sky had turned dusky gray when the filly stopped once more and lowered her head.

Jake halted, too. When he did, Sam held up the canteen, hoping he'd look back and remember he needed to stay hydrated.

He didn't take his eyes off the filly.

A lowered head could signal a weary horse, ready to give in and accept a leader, but Sam couldn't believe it had happened so soon, unless the filly was remembering that humans could be kind.

Sam stood in her stirrups for a better view. She tightened her reins. Chip slowed to a jolting jog, then stopped.

Sam saw a greenness on the plain where the filly had stopped.

Of course—water. The filly wasn't lowering her head to give in. She was smart enough to take a drink. Sam did the same, wishing Jake would, too.

Sam leaned low on Chip's neck, massaging the gelding's shoulder.

"You're a good, strong boy," she told the big horse. He stamped as if he agreed wholeheartedly. "I'd let Ace take a turn if I could, but he's back at the tent. Besides, it looks like we're about to have Jake back up in the saddle, and Ace can't carry double."

Ahead, Jake rested his hands on his hips. He still didn't look at Sam. He stretched one leg behind him, then the other. She'd bet he was trying to keep his muscles from cramping without moving toward the filly.

The pinto watched Jake. Head still lowered, she stared across the green pool, ears pointed right at him. Slowly, legs braced to run, she raised her head about halfway up. With water dripping from her muzzle, she took two steps toward him.

Oh, yeah, Sam thought as Jake retreated two

steps, *a teeny bit of progress.*

The filly tossed her head, then stood still. She gave a loud inquisitive snort, then jogged on.

"Guess I was wrong, Chip," Sam said, because Jake was following the filly once more.

It was full dark and Sam had let the monotony of the chase lull her into gazing blindly into the darkness, when she realized Jake had stopped up ahead of her.

"Water," he said.

Before Sam could hand it down to him, he placed his palms wide apart on Chip's shoulder and rested his forehead against the horse.

"Jake, are you all right?" She'd never seen him make such a weary gesture.

"No, it's killin' me, but at least I'm not doin' it under a blazing sun." He kept one hand against the horse as he took the canteen and leaned his head back to drink.

Sam watched his throat move in long gulps.

"Jake, you'd better stop," she cautioned. "When a horse has had this much exertion, you don't over-water him."

He ignored her, finished drinking, and peeled off his sweatshirt. He used it to mop his mouth, then the rest of his face.

Sam noticed he had a soft cotton rope knotted around his waist. Clearly he meant to put it around the filly's neck if she ever stopped.

"What's she doing?" he asked, since Sam was still facing the filly.

Sam peered through the darkness. The filly stood less than a quarter mile away. Her white markings were still visible, and she held her head to one side as if eavesdropping, while her long mane draped her shoulder.

"Just standing there," Sam said.

First, Jake began coughing. Next, he grabbed at his stomach.

"Cramps." He gasped, wrapping his arms around his stomach.

It wasn't like Jake to wait too long to drink, or to drink too fast and too much once he did.

"Oh, shoot," he said, with a mocking laugh at his own foolishness, "calves, too."

It took Sam a second to remember the painful muscle cramps she'd gotten some nights after playing basketball, but as Jake yanked up the legs of his sweatpants and rubbed at his calves, grimacing, she remembered and started to get down.

"No!" Jake pumped his arm in her direction. "Stay on. If she takes off, you've got to keep her in sight."

Sam stayed in the saddle and divided her attention between watching Jake walk two unsteady laps around Chip, and peering through the darkness toward the filly.

"She's still just watching us. Want something to eat?" she asked.

"I don't. It might make me puke," Jake said.

Sam gave a short laugh. This manhood initiation thing was showing her a whole other side of Jake Ely.

"You've been running for about two hours. Probably close to a marathon."

The faint praise cheered him up.

"Just give me one of those energy bars."

As Jake chewed, Sam glanced at the moon. It would be full in a couple of nights. If they were still out here, following this filly around, they wouldn't have time to get her ready for the race.

Sam glanced back at the filly.

"Jake," she said quietly. "Don't turn around, but I'm sure she's come toward us a few steps."

"What's she doing with her lips?"

Sam laughed again. "Are you getting delirious, Ely? It's dark. I can barely see something the size of a horse. I can't see her lips move."

Sam knew what he was waiting for, though. The mouthing movements of a weary, ready-to-give-in horse.

"I think we need to push her all night," Jake said, ending with a yawn.

"Much as I hate to admit it, I bet you're right," Sam said. "I've been thinking she might go back to the lake at dawn, and if there are no other horses there—"

"She might accept me," Jake finished.

"Or Chip," Sam suggested. "Do you want to ride now? I promise not to complain about your sweat."

"Thanks, Brat, but I'm gonna hold out a while." He turned back in the filly's direction. "Maybe she'll just let me walk up and put this rope around her neck and then we can all go in the tent and sleep."

"Don't count on it," Sam said, though the tent and a warm sleeping bag sounded like heaven. "Oh—"

She'd almost said "oh yuck" as Jake pulled the dirty sweatshirt back over his head, but then she realized how cold it had turned. She was glad to be wearing the coat she'd wanted to throw on the ground a while ago.

"'Oh' what?"

"I forget what I was going to say. Just go ahead and see how close she'll let you get."

Once Jake took five steps, the pinto resumed her run. In the moonlight, Sam watched the long, white legs carrying the filly across the range. They looked delicate in the moonlight, but the filly knew where she was going. Jake was more at risk than she was.

While they got a head start, Sam let Chip drop his muzzle down to sniff out some grass. Holding her reins in her teeth for just a few seconds, Sam pulled some jerky out of a sealed plastic pouch in the saddlebag. She ate it, washed it down with water, then clucked to Chip.

"Time to go, boy," she said. The good-natured Quarter horse blew through his lips, moved into a grudging jog, and kept up the pace until midnight.

Chapter Fifteen

*D*rumbeats, Sam thought.

She blinked and straightened. How could she have heard drumbeats?

Her back ached. She wished for her own Western saddle. Old as it was, it seemed comfy as a living-room chair compared to this little exercise saddle.

Those drumbeats must have pounded in her imagination. Probably, she'd been half dreaming.

No. There they were again. Not drumbeats, but hooves.

Chip stopped and neighed into the night.

Sam rubbed her eyes and listened. She forked her fingers through her hair, then pressed her nails against her scalp, trying to wake up.

Where am I? she wondered. She didn't have a clear idea of how the tribal lands looked on a map. Mac had said these fifty acres were fenced, though, so they couldn't get lost.

Night lay between her and the filly. Once in a while she glimpsed the black-and-white jigsaw pattern ahead. If Chip hadn't kept plodding, though, they might have lost her.

The night smelled like hay and wet rocks. If she had to guess, she'd say they'd circled back toward Monument Lake.

Still, there was no answer to Chip's neigh, so they rode on.

A half-hour later, Chip shied violently and nearly fell.

"Sorry," Jake called from the darkness. "I had to sit down a minute. There's this blister . . ."

While Sam comforted the tired Chip, Jake limped up, unbuckled the saddlebags, and rummaged around for a minute. He came up with a small flashlight and a Band-Aid.

"Mmmm, feels like heaven," he murmured as he sat on the bare ground, tending his foot.

"When you get that excited by a little bandage, it might be time to mount up," Sam said.

"Yeah," Jake said. "Give me a hand."

She kicked her boot free of the stirrup so Jake could use it. She grabbed his wrist and hauled him onto Chip.

The gelding gave a disgruntled snort, but that was all.

"He's a good horse, isn't he?" Jake asked in a sleepy voice. "Sweeter than his sister."

"You know what my dad says about Witch?" Sam joked. "The only safe place is on her back."

Jake chuckled and yawned. In minutes, he was dozing against Sam's back.

It was her job to stay awake, to make sure the filly didn't get a nap. The burden of responsibility stirred Sam. She adjusted her seat on Chip's back, feeling wide awake.

That was why she was pretty sure she didn't imagine the ghost horse.

Tatters of fog had drifted off the lake, obscuring all but sound.

The glowing blue-green numbers on her watch said three o'clock when she heard the clatter of many hooves, not four. She wasn't following the filly. Or, at least, not only the filly.

Had the Shoshone horses escaped? No, there weren't that many hooves.

Could the damp night air change sound?

Maybe, but as the fog floated apart, she saw a pure white tail drifting behind a trotting horse. But *black* streaked the pinto's tail and hours of pursuit had taken the zest from her trot. This was a different horse.

Chip didn't want to move closer, but when Sam tightened her legs and leaned forward, Chip obeyed.

A sudden squeal, pitched as if the horse were holding its breath, rushed at them. It was a stallion's territorial warning.

Could it be the Phantom? A gliding trot, a flowing tail, a pale mane wafting like a wave on the wind?

But the Phantom wouldn't ignore her, even if he wasn't always friendly. He'd been fierce and protective when he was courting Dark Sunshine. He'd been wild and threatening when he was drugged at the—wait.

Sam's tired mind finally focused. Could the Phantom be after Jake's filly? He was way out of his territory, and yet . . . she had to believe it was him or admit she'd had a hallucination.

A sudden hammering of hooves, like rocks bouncing off boulders, woke Jake.

"What's she doing?" he asked, groggily.

"She's okay. She hit some different footing," Sam said. And it was true, because now Chip's hooves clattered on stone. She could only hear his hooves and the filly's.

Where had the ghost horse gone?

On her very first day back in Nevada, after her accident, Dad had told her mustangs had hideaway trails no human knew.

She had to trust Dad's words, or believe the Phantom had blown away like mist on the wind.

Maybe she'd dreamed it. Sam hoped so, because she couldn't imagine what would happen if both Jake and the Phantom were after the same filly.

* * *

A wintry wind swept in just before dawn. Jake got off to run, just to keep warm. When he did, Sam let Chip rest.

I can't do this another night, she thought, *and neither can Chip. Maybe, if the sun comes out, Ace and I could do it tomorrow*. Or today. Whatever it was. Or whenever.

At last it was light enough to see the filly. Wide-eyed and nervous, she ran a few steps, stopped with lowered head, then turned toward Jake. Snorting and tossing her mane, she trotted in his direction.

Sam realized she'd pressed her hand flat against her chest, as if she could still her lurching heartbeat.

Even though the filly wheeled and bolted on faster than before, the change was coming.

At last they reached the lake. The filly treated it like home, wading in up to her knees. A sigh shuddered her lean body as she drank.

When Jake kept walking, following her into the water, she lifted her head to be sure of what she was seeing.

When he turned away, moving with a leisurely step as if he really was just strolling on the beach, the filly followed.

Sam's hands trembled on her reins.

When Jake stopped, the filly extended her head. She didn't look beaten, but curious. Could he be like the first humans she'd known? A kind one?

Without hesitating, Jake touched the white nose she offered, but Sam still held her breath.

Standing in front of the filly, as Jake was, could

be deadly. She could bolt forward or strike out, but she didn't.

Jake rubbed the inky forehead beneath her forelock. He fondled her silken black ears, stroked her long neck as he eased the rope around it and knotted it into a bowline.

All the time he was touching the filly, he spoke to her. Could Jake actually speak some Shoshone? Whatever he was saying, the filly understood every word.

Woodsmoke and bacon scented the morning air as they neared camp. Sam rode Chip. Jake led the pinto.

Although Sam and Jake savored the aromas and the crackle of a cookfire, the filly didn't. She braced her legs, ready to bolt.

"Here, now, girl, is that any way to act?" Jake chided. "It may not smell good to you, but I can't think of anything better."

He made her walk a few more steps before stopping.

"Why don't you go on into camp and bring me back a plate," he pretended to talk to the filly, though his words were for Sam. "I'll stay here with Star."

Sam felt her eyebrows rise at the name. It was sort of odd, since the filly had a white blaze on her forehead, not a star.

Mac welcomed Sam and told her to help herself to breakfast, but he hugged Chip and instantly began unsaddling him.

Sam stared at the food Mac had prepared, then looked at her watch for what must have been the hundredth time since yesterday. It was Saturday morning.

She and Chip and Jake had worked all night, but they'd caught the filly without hurt or harm, and almost without fear.

Yawning and slow, Sam prepared two plates and walked back to the clearing where Jake stood with the filly.

The pinto saw Sam and stumbled. One ear cupped toward Jake and the other swiveled toward Sam.

"It's okay, girl," Sam told her, but the filly disagreed.

Eyes wide, she swung her head from side to side. Was there just too much to be afraid of? Was she looking for something? Whatever concerned the filly, she didn't budge from her place close to Jake.

"No horse," he murmured to Sam. "You're off Chip and she doesn't recognize you."

Sam put Jake's plate down on a log that had been arranged here to make a trailside seat. Then, she backed away.

Her plate wobbled in her hand as she yawned yet again.

"Go take a nap, Brat. We can do without you for a little while."

Sam started to protest, then changed her mind.

As if he'd been expecting her, Mac held back the tent flap as she staggered back into camp.

"Just a few minutes," Sam said, as she crawled into her sleeping bag. "Just a few."

When Ace knocked the tent down, Sam woke in a tangle of nylon. It only took a few seconds to remember where she was and why.

Crawling out, she caught Ace's halter and stood.

She could see the water from here. A wooden canoe carried two fishermen to the middle of Monument Lake. A hot-pink kayak skimmed the water's surface, with only the dip, drip sound of the paddle to mark its passing.

The smell of piñon pines mixed with the cookfire's embers. She was alone with the horses. Chip dozed in a rope corral with one side down.

"Bad horse," Sam scolded Ace as she gave him a kiss on the nose. "Did you get bored?"

Sam repaired the corral, keeping Ace outside. Chip didn't even open his eyes.

Although every move caused a twinge of stiffness and pain, Sam saddled and bridled Ace, then grabbed a cold biscuit from a tin pan Mac had left on the wood table.

She started to mount up. Stepping into the stirrup was no big deal, but when she started to throw her leg over, she gasped.

Eight days. Eight days left and already it hurt to get into the saddle. She did it anyway and rode Ace toward the murmur of voices.

Sam could hardly believe what she saw when she got there.

Jake held a halter rope while he skimmed his hands over the filly's white back.

Each time he reached her flank, she flattened her ears and raised a hind hoof in warning.

Each time, he returned to pet her head and neck and start all over again.

"She's wearing a bridle," Sam said in amazement. "I miss everything."

"Not quite everything," Mac said. "He hasn't mounted her yet."

"I hope not," Sam said. "You're not going to, are you?" she asked Jake. "Not today."

"I'm not sure," Jake said. His eyes were red-veined from lack of sleep, but he looked happy. "Right now, I'm working on touch and—"

Distracted, he'd grazed the filly's haunch once more. She crouched back, positioning herself to strike with her front feet.

Sam moved Ace away from the filly. Her ears flicked forward as he went and the diversion kept her from attacking.

"No more of that, now," Jake crooned.

Drawn by his voice, the filly pressed forward until they were eye to eye. Sam couldn't believe it.

"What if I give Ace a refresher course," Sam said quietly. "You know, do all the things with him, that you do with her."

"Fine," Jake said. "But stay a little distance off, okay? If you put Ace right beside her she might think he's her herd instead of me. We don't have time for that."

"Got it," Sam said. "Now tell me about her name."

"Ah, yes," Mac said, and his smile seemed to fill his body as Jake explained.

"You'll think it's sappy," Jake said.

"Me?" Sam asked. "I won't, either."

"Okay. Look down here on her chest," Jake said. She did, and saw dozens of silver-white flashes on the filly's black hide.

"A star shower," Jake said meaningfully.

Sam's sleep-deprived mind took a minute to understand, but then she had it.

In the story Mac had told them, White Woman, who'd reached Dawnland first, had ridden a horse. Together, she and the horse had triggered a star shower that told everyone exactly where they belonged.

Was Jake hinting that the filly was helping him find where he belonged?

Jake's glare dared Sam to say something sentimental. This time, she gave him a break.

"I like it," Sam said simply, and Jake nodded.

For the rest of the day, they handled the horses, leading them over fallen logs and between trees whose trunks nearly touched.

Each time a horse shied, Sam and Jake turned away until the horse move forward and nudged or nuzzled to be noticed.

At last, Jake stood back at the end of the halter rope, and talked to Mac while he watched the filly.

"She's exhausted," Jake said. "And so am I, but I don't want to leave her in the rope corral and I'm afraid to tie her. What would you do, Grandfather?"

A second smile crossed Mac Ely's face, as if he saw that asking for his wisdom moved Jake another step closer to adulthood.

Mac sent Sam for Jake's sleeping bag. When she brought it, Jake looked as if he might beat it to the ground.

With Mac on watch, the filly was tied within sight, but not reach, of Jake's sleeping bag.

At once, the filly's head drooped, and her eyelids closed.

"She has white lashes on one eye and black on the other," Sam told Jake, but he was so tired, his nod put him off balance.

"She's asleep," he whispered a few seconds later. "I want her to rest. As soon as the moon rises, I'll lead her back into the water and see if she'll carry a rider."

Chapter Sixteen

"$\mathcal{I}$ have one chance to get it right," Jake said, as they finished a picnic dinner surrounded by horses.

Mac didn't contradict Jake with words, but he lifted one shoulder as if to say the filly might allow Jake to make a mistake or two.

"After me, she knows you best," Jake told Sam. "Will you hold the halter rope?"

Sam swallowed hard. Could she keep Star from running away if something frightened her? Sam had a mental image of the filly towing her like an upside-down water skier.

But she agreed anyway.

"Okay. Are we going to do the same thing we did with Blackie?"

Jake nodded, then interlaced his fingers and turned to Mac. "What would you teach her first, Grandfather?"

Sam could tell Jake really wanted advice. She wanted to suggest he use the red hawk feather she'd given him, but he might think she was being silly and superstitious.

He knew he had no time to waste and Mac's experience would be useful.

"You've already taught her to trust you. She was lonely and you became her friend. Now you must be worthy of her trust.

"Never hesitate. Never ask the horse to do what you're scared to do. Someone must rise to the top as leader and if you won't, the horse will."

It was true, Sam thought. Any time her mind wandered, Ace tried to take over. The first time she'd ridden Chip, he'd tried to go after Queen his own way. Even Strawberry, a lifelong cow horse, challenged Sam's authority.

At moonrise, they went to Monument Lake.

It seemed long ago that the Phantom had been Blackie, the colt she'd raised from birth, but Star looked just about the same age Blackie had been the day they'd led him into the river.

Sam remembered the flannel halter they'd made for Blackie, but Star seemed comfortable with the soft leather. She remembered Jake leading Blackie into the water so that she could pet him, talk with him, lean against him, then, oh so slowly, climb onto his back. Now it was her turn to hold the rope and Jake's turn to ride.

That first ride on Blackie had been gentle and perfect. The trouble had come later, when she'd tried to ride him through a gate on a windy day and he'd felt trapped and began bucking.

Sam shook her head. Jake was a better rider than she'd ever been. Besides that, Star wasn't Blackie.

The pinto filly made that clear right away. She refused to enter the water.

"Come on, little girl," Sam coaxed.

The filly wouldn't listen to sweet talk. First she flung her head high and backed away. Then, when Jake took the rope from Sam, the filly lowered her head, let her ears fall one to each side, and balked like a stubborn mule.

"I don't think she's going into the water," Sam said.

For the last few hours, Jake had been mild and quiet with his horse. Now the real Jake, understanding but in charge, was back.

He looked amused as he walked the filly up and down the shore.

"Last try," he said, leading Star toward the water again.

Her four legs braced wide as bedposts and she would not budge.

"Okay," Jake said, and with the reins and rope in

his left hand, he leaped for her back—and made it.

Star stood blinking. She'd forgotten all about the water. Something was on her back.

Jake touched her mane and petted her neck, talking. The filly swung her head around to look at Jake's left knee. Was she thinking about taking a bite?

Apparently not, because when Jake shifted his weight and stared down the shoreline, Star took a prancing step.

With hands and voice, Jake praised her, but there was amusement in his voice.

"You'll buck later, won't you girl? When I least expect—"

The filly ducked her head so low, her forelock hit the shore. With a mighty shove, she kicked her back hooves skyward. Jake nearly slid down her neck before she flung herself back, rising on her hind legs to paw at the moon.

Mac clapped and uttered a shout of such delight, that Sam hazarded a glance his way. This was the challenge Jake needed, and the old man was reveling in it.

Squealing, the filly actually took a step on her back hooves. If Jake lost his grip now, the filly would be gone.

Face buried in her mane, arms clinging to her neck, knees clamped hard against her shoulders, Jake stuck on as Star lunged and twisted, then darted down the shoreline.

Her hooves cut into the mud, strewing it in her wake.

She didn't run far. Sam saw her stop. When Jake asked her to, she turned.

Pretending she'd been insulted, the filly shook her variegated mane and trotted back to camp, following Jake's requests as if she'd been doing it all her life.

Heaven was spring vacation with only horses on her mind, Sam decided.

It was Monday afternoon and Star hadn't exploded again. She still shied and threatened to bolt, but she didn't seem to have a mean bone in her body.

Each day, Sam and Jake tested the horses by riding over strange footing, under low-hanging branches, along narrow trails. They had Mac wave a blanket, clang a pot lid with a metal spoon, and howl like a coyote. The horses were learning to expect anything.

Star grew calmer, but instead of becoming dependent on Jake, her wild personality showed through. Once she grabbed Ace's tail in her teeth, gave it a yank, then walked slowly away, as if she'd had nothing to do with it.

Later the same day, she cautiously mouthed a lock of Jake's hair. He looked surprised, but stood still, waiting to see what she did.

Star gave his hair a gentle tug. Then, when he turned laughing to face her, she swung her head away and pretended to be studying a tree.

"The spirit of the horse remains," Mac said, "if the rider doesn't fight to replace it with his own."

On Tuesday, twilight had spread over the range and Jake and Mac had left Sam to pony Star back to camp. Being led by a rider on another horse was a skill Star was still learning.

All at once, Sam got the finger-down-the-spine *watched* feeling she'd had before.

Was there a cougar? Sam gazed up at the tree-tops. Here in the cottonwoods a cougar could hide, but Jake would have noticed even the faintest cat track.

Ace and Star snorted in the same instant and their necks craned toward the sound of hooves.

The Phantom trotted out of the cottonwoods. Neck arched, shoulders muscled beneath silver satin skin, he trotted directly up to Star.

Oh, no. Sam jerked the lead rope, pulling the filly's head around. Star planted her feet more firmly. Sam knew the filly was stubborn enough to resist.

Ace danced in place, eager to greet the stallion who'd been his herd leader. Sam sat into him, reminding Ace she needed his help.

"You've got plenty of mares." She scolded the Phantom, although her hopes weren't high that he'd listen. "Leave Star alone."

The stallion's ears flicked in her direction, but that was all. He and Star were locked in a stare.

The filly quit balking. She pranced and played, throwing herself to the end of the rope, trying to go with the stallion as he backed away. Sam's grip started to slip and she used both hands on the rope, hoping she could keep Ace steady with her knees.

And then Star lunged.

"No!" Sam shouted. She fought being jerked out of the saddle, but she'd have to choose. Hold the rope or grab the saddle horn.

If she let Star go, Jake would never forgive her.

"Jake!" Sam shouted. If the Phantom saw other humans, maybe he'd go. "Jake!"

Sam's shouts were all the excuse Star needed. She reared high on her hind legs, and Ace backed out of her way.

Sam's grip on the rope loosened as Star pulled it across her palm in searing, hot pain. No matter how she tried, Sam couldn't hold on.

She'd lost the rope, but the filly was still there.

Breathing hard, Sam tried to think. The rope trailed behind the filly, but Star was still playing. She didn't know she was free.

"Get her, Ace," Sam told him. "Cut her out."

The filly was no steer, and there was no herd to separate her from, but Ace knew what to do.

His body settled lower to the ground. Sam let her reins go slack, and he slipped between the stallion and Star. Even though it was dangerous to turn his back on the Phantom, the gelding obeyed.

He wouldn't let Star past. He blocked her like he

would a cranky cow. As Sam watched, the filly stayed centered between Ace's ears. He had no intention of letting Star get away.

Suddenly, Star gave up.

She swished her tail and nickered. *I was just having fun*, the filly seemed to say, and now she was ready to go back to the rope corral.

Sam sighed. Everything was going to be all right.

But the Phantom wasn't giving up. With flattened ears, the stallion brushed past Ace and shoved the filly with his head.

He wasn't playing games. He'd decided Star was his. When she hesitated, he gave her a bite on the rump. She squealed and bolted.

"No!" Sam shouted again. She waved her hand in the Phantom's face.

He was blind to her. It was spring and he had to gather as many mares as he could to build up his herd against other stallions' raids.

Ace sensed the Phantom's mood change. He scrambled to avoid the stallion's slashing hooves.

Ace knew he was losing, but he wasn't stupid. He let the stallion have Star, then turned and sprinted, trying to cut her off once more.

But Star was running scared. As the stallion herded, nipped, and whinnied behind her, her long white legs reached out. She galloped in the direction he herded.

Sam heard shouting behind her, but she kept after the two horses.

Cutting through the trees and brush, they spotted a wilderness camper. He waved, but Sam ignored him. If she lost Star, Jake would hate her. He'd think she'd allowed the Phantom to do as he pleased. He'd never believe the truth.

Out of the narrow neck of the tribal lands she chased the horses. Ace lined out like a greyhound, unused to losing the animal he was trying to cut out.

Past hills that looked like crumpled pink paper they ran, and suddenly Sam recognized the terrain.

What had Mac said? Or was it Jake? A finger of the tribal lands extended between Lost Canyon and Arroyo Azul.

"Go, boy!" Sam leaned low on Ace's neck, letting his black mane whip her eyes. If the stallion got the filly into Arroyo Azul, he'd take her down the secret tunnel that led to his valley. She'd be lost to Jake, forever.

"Careful, boy, careful," Sam whispered to Ace.

They'd been following Star and the Phantom for what seemed like hours. Sam didn't risk a minute looking at her watch. It didn't matter; she'd follow as long as she could hear them picking their path through sagebrush, between boulders.

Ace felt her urgency, and he'd sweated up almost immediately. He charged uphill faster than she would have pushed him, and each time the narrow ledge trails leveled, he wanted to run.

She kept watching on her right. She knew the shaley path down to Arroyo Azul was coming up. Any minute now, she'd see it. With luck, the two horses would take it slowly enough that she could catch them and grab Star's lead rope. What she didn't want was to fight the filly on one of these narrow, cliffside trails.

All at once, she hit a dead end. Her path was blocked by a huge rock face with a crack running across it. Water seeped out, too, and she recognized it.

She'd ridden through Lost Canyon. She was on the opposite end, near War Drum Flats.

Why hadn't she seen the path down to Arroyo Azul?

She let Ace take a quick drink, then turned him. It didn't matter how. She'd missed the downhill trail. She'd have to backtrack.

She did it, but she kept Ace reined in.

Her spirits crashed. There was no point in hurrying.

She'd be too late. The horses would be long gone and she'd have to take all the blame for Star's escape.

Chapter Seventeen

Sam heard Chip's hooves coming before she saw him.

It was almost dark and Jake's hair blew in the wind, giving him a fearsome silhouette.

"Don't rush," he shouted. "He's already got her."

Jake's words slashed her like physical pain, but she didn't take it in silence.

"Ace is winded. We passed the trail down to Arroyo Azul. Somehow—I don't know. It's here somewhere." She gestured toward the edge. "It goes down, but I didn't see it. If I couldn't find it in the light, I'm worried that now, in the dark . . ."

"Pretty hopeless, isn't it?" Jake's voice was sarcastic, as if she hadn't tried.

"I did everything I could to catch them!"

Jake shrugged.

"I *did*!" she insisted. "Look at Ace. He's lathered up and exhausted. Would I do that to him for nothing?"

"For nothing?" Jake asked. "Or for your precious Phantom?"

Something invisible and frigid clamped around her.

"I'm not lying. I did my—"

"Take me to his hideout." Jake's voice stopped her before she could finish.

"That's what I was trying to tell you," Sam said. "There's a way down to Arroyo Azul and I couldn't find it."

"Take me in from the other direction, then. From the River Bend side. We'll go back to camp and Mac can drive us."

He was daring her. Every syllable of each word told Sam he knew she wouldn't do it.

Jake believed she was lying and the only way she could prove him wrong was by betraying the Phantom.

"I can't," she said, at last.

In the deserted canyon, with rock set like shelves all around, her voice sounded hollow and alone.

Sam didn't see the reins move or Jake shift, but he spun Chip and sent him back the way they'd come, back to Monument Lake, without Star.

❀ ❀ ❀

A campfire burned and Mac sat beside it, but he wasn't alone.

"Dad!" Sam shouted.

He caught her as she slipped down from Ace, then hugged her tight.

Was Dad surprised at the way she clung to him? Was he staring over her head at Mac or Jake? She didn't care.

Sam wanted to stay there forever, hidden in Dad's arms. Jake hadn't said a word as they'd ridden back. He'd forced her to choose between him and the Phantom, and she'd chosen her horse.

If it had been life or death, she would have chosen differently. She knew that. But maybe Jake didn't. Still, this wasn't life or death.

Star might come back on her own.

Jake could ride Witch in the race.

Or think of another manhood test.

But once she revealed the Phantom's hiding place, she couldn't take it back.

"Ready to go home for a little break?" Dad asked. He set her away from him, but only to the length of his arms.

"I don't know," Sam said. She wet her lips and turned to ask Jake, but she only saw his back as he ducked into the tent.

"Jacob!" Mac's voice was like a whiplash.

Jake lifted the tent flap. "Yes, Grandfather?"

"What will you do next?"

A lone cricket, braving the cool spring night, sang from the cottonwoods. When its solo ended, Jake still hadn't spoken.

"Jake, I'm sorry," Sam said again. "I did everything I could to hold her, but she reared and . . ."

Jake didn't interrupt, but Sam was listening so intently, she heard his lips part. She stopped to hear what he'd say.

"I'm going out at daylight to track her. No sense in you staying around."

That was it, then.

What had she expected him to say? He was telling her he'd go on without her. Telling her he didn't need her. Asking her to go away.

"You go get your stuff, then," Dad said. "I'll load Ace. I expect he could use a little time at home, too."

Jake stepped aside, letting her into the tent, very carefully not brushing her sleeve.

He stood at the flap while she crammed her belongings into her backpack.

Why was he just standing there, watching? Why didn't he say something? She worked quickly, but he had plenty of time to apologize. He didn't.

The zipper on her backpack sounded loud and final as she ducked past the tent flap.

She'd already started toward Dad's truck when Jake called after her.

"Sam?"

Her heart hammered so loud, she didn't know if she could hear him, but she turned, biting her lip to keep from saying anything dumb.

"You forgot this," he said.

For a minute she couldn't tell what it was. This far from the campfire, the light was dim, but then something soft grazed her fingertips. As soon as she grasped it, she knew what it was.

Jake had returned the glossy red-brown hawk's feather that she'd given him. For luck.

Things weren't so bad, back at the ranch. If she hadn't felt heartsick and nervous, everything might have been fine.

She decided to give Ace and Sweetheart a try in the ten-acre pasture. At worst, she'd rescue Ace five minutes after she turned him out. At best, he'd fit into the saddle horse herd and rekindle his friendship with Dark Sunshine.

Instantly, the buckskin perked up. She loped to Ace and seemed to make little darting figure eights with her muzzle. She trotted alongside him, uttering nickers of joy. Neck arched, she kept bowing her head as if telling the others to look at her new friend.

When they did, the best of all possible things happened: nothing. They weren't mean, aggressive, or excited. They barely noticed Ace was back.

Sam spent most of Thursday alone.

Brynna was at work and Dad was readying Nike

and Jeepers-Creepers for the race. Although Gram clearly knew something was wrong, she didn't pump Sam for information, even when she turned down a chance to go back out to Monument Lake.

She knew Jen and Ryan were working with their horses, so she didn't call. At least that was the excuse she gave Gram, but Sam knew it was something more. She was afraid she might confess what had happened with Jake and Star. Her feelings were still too raw to talk about, so she didn't take that chance.

Then, Jen called her.

"Things are really crazy around here," Jen whispered. "My dad stood up to Slocum about the buffalo."

"What about them?"

"They arrived on Tuesday and they're really hard to handle. Linc hasn't set up a big enough pasture and Dad insists they can't be put out with the cattle until they've been in quarantine.

"And Dad's refusing to truck them over to Mrs. Allen's for the race. He says they're entirely unpredictable."

"Sorta like cows?" Sam asked.

When Jen squeaked in surprise, Sam smiled for the first time in days.

"I can't believe I said that," Jen recalled. "They're really kind of ferocious. Ryan thinks they're great, but Sky doesn't like them at all."

Sam got chills at the way Jen said it. She really sounded scared.

"Good for your dad, then," Sam said. "I can't picture Linc bringing them over by himself, can you?"

"To tell you the truth, I can picture him doing just about anything." Jen covered the phone's mouthpiece, to talk with someone else, but Sam still heard her say, "I'm *not* biting the hand that feeds me, Mom!"

For a few seconds, Jen and Lila bickered over Jen's criticism of Slocum.

"All right, Mom, I'm getting off." Jen laughed. "Gotta go, Sam. Hey, see you at the races!"

Sam had worked Ace early in the morning and groomed him afterward, but she went out to groom him anyway.

He didn't need it. The gelding was thriving on the extra attention he'd received this week. His coat glowed red gold and his black mane and tail were silky.

Just the same, she curried him and told him what she'd been afraid to tell anyone else.

"I want to go get her, Ace. She's up there with the Phantom and I'd like to go get her, but there are at least two things wrong with that."

The mustang bobbed his head as if he understood, but she told him anyway.

"One, the Phantom might not let me take her. I couldn't stand battling him. He might never come to me again. Two." Sam sighed. "Jake might track me! I've seen him track across bare rock. Do you know that Quinn has called here twice, asking what I'm up to? Don't you just know Jake has him spying on me?

"But if I don't get her back, there goes my chance to be in the race, my chance to show Dad I have some riding skills. And you are doing so well," she said, hugging the mustang's neck.

Sam stood there thinking. The carpenters had made lots of progress on the barn, and she watched them while she concentrated.

Just then, Ross rode in on Tank. The big gelding was limping.

"What's wrong?" Sam called.

"Threw a shoe," he said, and when he looked more sheepish than usual, Sam remembered Dad had turned the shoeing chore over to Ross that first day they'd talked about the race.

Sam shrugged with an understanding grin and expected Ross to disappear. Instead, he took a breath, expelled it, and managed another sentence.

"That filly of Jake's a paint?"

Sam nodded, and hope crowded out every other feeling. Ross never wasted a word in idle conversation.

"Saw a strange paint just 'cross the river."

"Oh my gosh, Ross, that is so cool. *So* cool!" She grabbed the cowboy's upper arms and might have kissed him in joy, but he looked so startled she released him. "Thanks!"

Sam saddled Ace. She got a rope from the half-ruined tack room and tied it onto her saddle. It could work.

She ran into the kitchen.

"Gram, I'm taking Ace out for a little while."

She already had the door open again when Gram's voice stopped her.

"You're not going up into the mountains after the filly, are you?"

Sam shook her head. "Nope, I'm hoping she'll come to me."

If I only I had my horsehair bracelet, Sam thought.

She knew it was superstitious, but she had a feeling that once she crossed to the wild side of the river, its magic would draw the filly to her.

You didn't need it for the Phantom. The whisper came in her own voice and she realized it was true. She didn't need a magic bracelet. The power she had over the Phantom was her own. And if she could communicate with him, she might be able to connect with the filly. All she needed was a chance.

Where was she? Sam stared so hard her eyes already burned.

Even though the sandspit jutting out into the river made it possible to ride across La Charla, it took thirty minutes to ride from River Bend Ranch to the Phantom's trail through the stairstep mesas.

"We're not going up, boy," she said when Ace

tugged at the bit. "I don't know where Jake is, but he'd follow our tracks for sure."

Instead, they loped back and forth, letting any animal around know they were there.

She was determined to be in that race. If Jake didn't have Star, he could ride Chip. She'd *make* him ride Chip.

The Quarter horse had shown his stamina and will during that long night they'd chased the filly. He could certainly run a seven-and-a-quarter-mile race.

A lonely neigh made Ace spin on his heels.

The pretty pinto had sighted them, but she didn't know the path down. She picked her way slowly through the sagebrush and shale.

"Star, pretty Star," Sam called.

The filly had lost her leather halter and the rope trailing from it. This wasn't going to be easy.

Sam remembered what Mac had said about not asking your horse to do something you're not brave enough to do.

Although her palm was still ripped and red from the last time she'd tried to hold onto the black-and-white filly, Sam knew that if Star came to her, she'd be brave enough to slip a loop over her head and never let go.

Chapter Eighteen

A racket started up on the road that ran past River Bend Ranch and paralleled the La Charla River.

Instead of fleeing, the filly's ears pricked up and she watched it come with such intensity that Sam looked, too.

Mac Ely's red Scout wagon was headed toward Three Ponies Ranch, dragging the horse trailer carrying Chip.

Sam was still deciding what to do when the Scout stopped. It was at least two miles away, but Sam knew what was about to happen.

She glanced back at the filly. Star hadn't come closer but, ears flicking, she kept watching the small figure that was Jake.

She loosed a high, wild neigh and trotted forward.

She knew him!

When Sam looked back at Jake, he'd crossed the river. Even though he wore jeans that had to be wet from crossing, he was running.

The filly advanced more cautiously, but the steps of her trot grew longer, and then she broke into a lope.

Sam tightened Ace's reins, leaving Jake alone to greet his filly.

He had no rope, no saddle, or bridle, but when Star reached him, she stopped. Head lowered, she nibbled his hair. When she raised her head again, nodding, Jake slid his hand along her side. Then, with a hop and a handful of mane, he jumped onto her bare back.

The filly circled nervously, and gave a few half-hearted bucks to punish him for their parting.

But when Jake leaned low on her neck, she forgave him. His black hair mixed with her wild mane and Star lunged into a gallop. They ran along the river, away from Sam, until they were out of sight.

On race day, Sam pulled on a sweatshirt and her softest old jeans to go downstairs for breakfast. Still yawning, she entered the kitchen and saw Dad sitting at the table drinking coffee. With Jake.

"Am I late?" she gasped. Every nerve crackled with something like electricity. If she'd overslept, after all of this . . .

"No," Jake said, as he pushed back from the table.

Dad stood before Jake could, made an excuse about checking water troughs, and left them alone.

Sam had a bad feeling about what was coming next.

"I'm sorry about that stuff I said in Lost Canyon," Jake said.

Sam's throat constricted. Her chest ached all over again, remembering how he'd accused her of letting the Phantom steal Star. She held onto the back of a chair, unable to respond.

"Last night," Jake went on, "I did this meditation thing Dad told me about. You lay out four sticks, one for each direction. You know, east, west . . ."

"Yeah, I've heard of them," Sam joked, hoping to erase Jake's serious expression.

He only shook his head. "Anyway, I sat in that square and thought for hours. I wanted to focus on the race, but I only realized what a jerk I'd been to you."

"It's over," she began, but his look of frustration stopped her from adding more.

"Here's what kinda came to me." Jake laced his fingers together and stared at them, instead of looking at her. "Whatever it is in your head or heart that made you not betray the Phantom's hideout, it's the same thing that made you stand up for me."

"When did I stand up for you?" Sam asked.

"You could have told Mac and your dad how I acted and what I said. You didn't. You let them think I was succeeding at this manhood thing."

"You are, Jake," Sam said, softly.

Apologies came hard to Jake, but his sudden, fearful look said he found her compliment even harder to accept.

Jake folded his arms and cleared his throat. "So that's all. Now, if you don't mind, I'd feel better about riding in this race if I could have my feather back."

The starting line of the race had become a carnival. At least a hundred people had gathered to ride or watch. Girl Scouts had set up a cookie booth. The Darton High Art Club was painting children's faces and the Methodist Women's Society was making a pancake breakfast.

Wearing a red shirt, jeans, the new chaps Dad and Brynna had given her for an early birthday present, and her old brown Stetson, Sam enjoyed the activity as she and Jake led Ace and Star toward the other horses.

Jake wore his usual shirt and jeans, but Star Shower tossed her head, showing off the red hawk feather braided into her mane.

The race had drawn twenty teams.

"Forty horses. One team made the trip from Canada. Hard to believe, isn't it? On short notice, I think Mrs. Allen's doing pretty good, don't you?" Sam said. "I mean, people have only known about it for—"

"You're doing it again," Jake said quietly.

"Doing what? Babbling because I'm nervous?" Sam asked.

"Sounds like it," Jake said.

When Star startled at the flap of the plastic flags used to mark the course, Jake swung onto her back and rode her in a small circle.

"Maybe I'll mount up, too," Sam told Ace.

All the horses had been checked by Dr. Scott and most were massed at the starting line. Now, she and Jake joined them.

On the way, they passed Dad and Brynna. They looked pretty serious, though they were still claiming half the reason they were riding was to keep an eye on Sam.

Katie Sterling and her father rode tall black horses. Sam had heard someone say that they were Standardbreds.

Star shied as an electronic screech was followed by Mrs. Allen's voice on a fuzzy loudspeaker.

"Last call, riders. All contestants should be lined up at the starting line. It's now or never, folks."

Sam held her breath for a minute, but she couldn't keep quiet.

"Don't Ryan and Jen look great," Sam whispered to Jake.

"You know," he drawled, "I was just sayin' to myself, that Ryan is one—"

"Shut up, Jake."

Roman and Sky slipped into place about three teams down. Sam leaned forward and waved at Jen. She waved back, but her hands were full with her mount and Sam could hear Ryan's accented voice as he gave Jen nonstop directions.

For once, Jen needed them.

Sky's dark brown body gleamed as if it had been oiled. He minced sideways, flattening his ears at other horses. Once, he lashed his heels at Roman, but most of the other contestants stayed away.

"Roman's making mustangs look good," Sam told Ace, but then something on the obstacle course ahead caught her eyes.

She studied it as Mrs. Allen's voice boomed over the microphone again. "The siren will take the place of a starter's pistol."

"What's that?" she asked Jake, pointing.

The field ahead was scattered with all kinds of distractions designed to test horsemanship skills.

There was a sawhorse topped with flashing red lights, a truck with its backup sound turned on, and two troops of cub scouts. One group carried helium-filled balloons. The other played kazoos.

Even Jake's brothers, Quinn and Bryan, were there, pounding a beat on authentic Native American drums. Mac stood by them, looking proud, while Jake's parents and Gram watched from the sidelines.

Telephone poles had been laid on the ground to mark off lanes for the first quarter mile of the race.

"What's what?" Jake asked.

"That big truck. Please tell me it's not filled with Slocum's buffalo."

"Doesn't matter if it is," Jake said. "We're about to go."

A Darton County sheriff turned on the siren in his police car for one loud whoop. Chills covered every inch of Sam's skin and the race began.

"Good boy, good boy," Sam crooned to Ace.

His ears flicked forward, back, and to each side, but he passed the bobbing balloons without a snort and navigated the space between the logs without a single misstep. He hesitated at the bleating kazoos, but when Sam glanced around, she saw he was having far less trouble than most horses.

Ace made it through the obstacles in first place, and stood fidgeting as he waited for Star.

A pair of riders on matched chestnuts clearly hadn't prepared their horses for chaos. One horse was threatening to rear and his partner was already bucking.

Katie Sterling and her father dashed by, and then a couple that Sam didn't recognize galloped past on lean ponies in English gear.

Then Jake caught up.

"She did not like that heart-shaped balloon," Jake muttered as the horses fell into a lope.

Sam looked back once more. One rider down. A number of horses were shying or refusing to pass obstacles that seemed especially terrifying.

"We don't have time to look back," Jake shouted, and this time, Sam followed his order without protest.

Leaving Deerpath Ranch, they galloped across the range for La Charla.

Neither horse balked at the water crossing, although one of the ponies' riders stood knee-deep and drenched, remounting in midstream.

As soon as Sam and Jake were through the river, the trail turned south. Ace stretched out, loving this flat stretch that took them past River Bend Ranch.

Star caught his excitement and ran beside him.

Sam looked to her right. Jake rode Star bareback, with only a lightweight bridle. Though the filly's eyes were wide and her head whipped from side to side, enjoying the scenery, she ran almost in step with Ace.

The course had just turned east at the Gold Dust Ranch when Sam heard hooves thundering up from behind.

Jake had told her not to look back, not to lose her concentration on the trail ahead, but she couldn't help it.

Roman's flaring nostrils and level head were just feet away. The mustang looked free again. Ryan lay low on his neck, letting the gelding run.

Jen was half a length behind, but suddenly Sky's legs reached ahead of Roman's and he swept past Ace.

In wordless agreement, Sam and Jake tucked their horses in behind Jen and Ryan. When the other horses tired, they'd pass them.

The black Standardbreds kept the lead, but Jen and Ryan were close behind.

Sky should be tired, Sam thought. All the energy he put into misbehaving at the start would have to tell on him.

Far behind her, Sam heard a scream. *Don't look back*, she ordered herself, and it was a good thing she didn't. Just ahead, one of the blacks was falling behind. It was the one ridden by Katie Sterling's dad. As she reined in, staying with her dad and his horse, Jen and Ryan flew into first place.

"After them!" Jake shouted.

Star and Ace seemed to understand. They split, one passing to each side of Roman and Sky, and galloped into the lead, dashing across the white expanse of War Drum Flats.

Another scream and more commotion made Sam and Jake both look back.

What could be going on? Sam's eyes scanned the horses and riders, the familiar terrain, and suddenly she saw it.

A huge brown buffalo parted the running horses with his horned and curly head. He ran as fast as the horses!

Jake nodded right and Star veered off. Ace swung after her and they let the buffalo take the lead.

He didn't want it. Maybe he recognized Jen or Ryan or Sky, or maybe it was just coincidence that the buffalo swerved toward those from his new home.

Sky panicked. Avoiding the charge, he tried to rear, but Jen forced him down. Tail and legs stiff with fear, Sky swerved into Roman. The mustang stumbled, but didn't fall. Sky's eyes rolled white and his breathing was so loud, Sam heard it over the pounding of hooves. But Roman and Sky were shoulder to shoulder now. They looked safe and the buffalo was falling behind.

"Go for it!" Sam called to Jake, and Ace and Star burst ahead with renewed energy.

The finish line at Deerpath Ranch was just ahead. They could make it. They could win!

All at once, there was a bawling sound and a crash.

Sam looked back in time to see Sky fall.

"Jen!" Sam screamed, and she felt Ace hesitate beneath her.

Jake began talking to Star as she hopped, threatening to buck. He tightened his reins. The pinto shook her head wildly, eager to run on, but he didn't let her. Sam did the same thing, but Ace was ready to slow.

Jake and Sam turned their mounts in a wide circle, back toward Jen.

Jen was on the ground, trying to stand. She gripped one of her split reins and got to her feet just as Sky scrambled up.

The black Standardbreds flashed past but Sam was watching Jen.

Jen's palms were bloody and so was one of her cheeks. Through the ripped knees of her jeans, Sam saw more blood.

Sky neighed and backed to the end of his reins, shaking his head and then, Sam saw Ryan.

Roman was slinging his head from side to side, fighting the reins as Ryan ordered him to run straight. Didn't he see Jen in his path?

"Mount up!" Sam shouted.

If Roman didn't trample Jen, another horse could. She'd be safer in the saddle.

Jen used the back of her hand to bat one white-blond braid away from the corner of her mouth.

"I'm fine," she shouted at Sam. "Go on, go on."

Her shout pushed Sky over the edge. He began

bucking, and when Jen tripped, then used her hands to cover her head, he broke loose and ran after the leaders. But a riderless horse couldn't win.

Sam's mind spun. Only the black Standardbreds had passed. With Jen's horse lost and Ryan battling Roman, she and Jake could pass the Standardbreds. They already had once. They could win.

There were two riders coming up behind them. They'd have to hurry.

But she couldn't leave Jen out here, on foot. With bison on the loose, Jen was in danger.

"Here!" Sam said. She kicked her boot free of the stirrup and reached down for Jen.

Jen looked back and saw Ryan fighting Roman. Foam flew from the liver chestnut's gaping mouth and Sam saw Jen give up. She grabbed Sam's hand and jammed her foot in the stirrup.

Sam coughed against the dust, but just as Jen swung up behind her, she saw the two approaching riders more clearly. They were Dad and Brynna.

Dad's questioning expression turned into astonishment, then pride.

Sam waved him on. "Someone in the family might as well win!"

"Sure?" he shouted.

"We're fine!" Sam reined Ace next to Jake and Ryan. Star and Roman were trotting together as if they'd been schooled to do it. "Just watch out for the buffalo."

Dad touched his hat brim in a sort of salute, then

he and Brynna galloped on.

"You can still do it," Jen said, slipping down from Ace.

"What?" Sam asked.

Jen bolted toward Ryan, and stood near him.

They looked fine, Sam thought. Her heart pounded hard in her chest and Ace stood tall.

"Yes," Ryan said, "thanks, but we'll take it slow from here. You might as well go on."

Ryan's gratitude was all they needed to set Star and Ace into a last bolt for the finish line.

Low on the filly's neck, Jake's black hair mixed with her mane, and the scarlet feather might have been his.

Sam leaned further forward, cheek pressed to Ace's neck. Wind whipped tears into her eyes, but she was smiling.

Honking horns and shouts came from the finish line as the Sterlings won. Brynna and Dad were right behind them, a certain second.

Third place wasn't so bad, Sam thought, especially when the horses didn't know they hadn't won.

Ace pranced beside Star and the filly tossed her head, wide-mouthed with excitement as they rode past Linc Slocum who was having a serious conversation next to a Darton County sheriff's squad car.

Jake's family stood with Gram, Brynna, and Dad. The Ely brothers had gathered together and began talking excitedly as Sam and Jake approached.

"Buffalo hunt, man," Bryan shouted to Jake.

"Slocum's in trouble for failure to keep track of his buffalo."

Mrs. Ely tried to shush him, but Quinn took over.

"Only seven escaped, but we get to ride after 'em! Is that cool, or what?"

Nate had borrowed three horses. At a hammering trot, he returned riding one and leading two.

He passed Ryan leading Roman and walking with Jen, who was mounted again on Sky. Sam grinned at the way her bedraggled friend was lecturing Sky and ordering him to behave.

Bryan swung into the saddle of a rose-gray Arab. Quinn mounted Jeepers-Creepers and the Appaloosa tossed his head, still ready to run.

"Let's go, man, let's go!" Bryan yelled.

Before he joined them, though, Jake turned to Ryan.

He rubbed the back of his neck and, for the first time all day, Star sidestepped and tossed her head.

She felt her rider's nerves, Sam thought. What was Jake about to say to Ryan?

"Your mustang did great," Jake said.

"Thank you," Ryan replied in astonishment. "Really, thank you very much."

Mac watched with quiet satisfaction, nodding.

Jake rode a little closer and Star rubbed her neck against Ace's. The gelding blew through his lips, stamped, and lowered his head.

Sam met Jake's eyes. She wanted to go on the buffalo hunt. Jake wouldn't mind, but Ace was tired.

"Jake!" Nate shouted.

A hundred yards away, all three Ely brothers were circling on rocking, rambunctious horses. Only Jake was still here.

They should go together and she should stay.

"What are you waiting for?" Sam asked.

Jake smiled, gave Star a touch with his heels, and the filly swung around. Seeing the other running horses, she leaped with all four feet off the ground, then set off at a gallop.

As Sam dismounted slowly, watching them go, Dad walked up, leading Nike.

"I'm proud of you, honey." He hugged her with one arm.

Brynna jogged up on foot.

"I just heard the buffalo have been sighted, clumped in a herd, and heading for the river."

"I think they heard, too," Sam said, laughing.

Jake and his brothers were yelling, riding full out in a noisy band.

"Do you know," Mac confided to Dad, "I thought I'd be long, long passed over before I saw all my boys grown up and on a buffalo raid. But there it is, right before my eyes."

They all watched as Star bolted ahead, carrying Jake.

With the wind in his hair and sun on his back, he looked like a part of the filly.

Sam watched them out of sight. Even when they'd vanished, she couldn't stop smiling.

From
Phantom Stallion
∽ 11 ∾
UNTAMED

The first thing Sam noticed as they came to the edge of a wide plain was the shadow. Snake Head Peak cast a column of darkness over the sagebrush and bunch grass-covered flat.

Sam had just decided they were on a wild goose chase when something moved. Suddenly, she wasn't looking at a monochrome landscape.

A herd of grazing mustangs and pronghorn covered the flat.

Ace and Silly snorted and danced, but the wild animals had long since picked up the scent of the intruders.

Antelope and wild horses.

Sam's hand fell from the reins, about to touch her mother's note. Ace was too spooked already to risk rustling paper where he couldn't see it. Besides, she didn't need to look. She knew what the note said. Her pulse pounded and her eyes swept the plain, looking for danger.

The brown and white antelope had black horns that seemed perfectly aligned with their dark eyes. They were small, maybe three feet tall, and they'd frozen statue still among the horses.

There. As two blood bay mares showed themselves amid the mustang herd, Sam's heart bounded up with joy. Those two ran with the Phantom's band. She couldn't see him, but the great silver stallion had to be nearby.

Ace bolted forward, reminding Sam that this had once been his herd. She tightened her reins and Ace stopped, but his tail moved in a resentful swish.

Some silent signal flashed among the pronghorn. Like multicolored popcorn, they bounded, not up, but in long leaps, from a dozen spots within the herd of mustangs.

Sam couldn't catch enough breath to speak to Jen.

The pronghorn were coming this way. Slender and graceful as deer, they turned so she could see the cinnamon swatches on their backs. Their cheeks and chests were milky white.

Once separated from the mustang herd, they joined together. *For safety*, Sam thought. Their leaps were amazingly broad and they'd moved so close that Sam could see some had faces marked with broad black bands.

Then they turned.

Like a flock of birds, they moved as one until she could only see their white rumps fleeing across the range, away from the horses.

"I can't believe . . ." Sam began.

She was thinking of Mom and the notes she'd left

behind. Something about the antelope and mustangs had worried her mother, but Sam only saw their beauty.

A flash of silver caught Sam's attention. Ace bunched beneath her and then she heard a stallion's scream.

The Phantom rushed through his mares, scattering them as he galloped.

Sam had seen this charge before. She searched for an intruding stallion.

"There," Jen said, pointing.

Sam saw the clump of sagebrush, but no horse.

"What are you — ?"

The flicker of brightness, at ground level, could have been a match, or light bouncing off a mirror, but then a crack of lightning rolled through the desert air.

"Run!" Jen shouted. She clapped her heels to Silly's sides and leaned low as the mare surged from a nervous walk into a full gallop. Jen's white-blond braids mixed with the palomino's flaxen mane.

Sam didn't follow, though her chaotic thoughts finally focused. That crack had been a rifle shot. There was no way she'd leave the Phantom here alone, to face a gunman.

But a man with a rifle wasn't a mustang's natural enemy. The Phantom shouldn't charge; he should run.

The rest of his herd fled as a big honey-brown mare led them after the antelope. Far out on the plain, they were nothing more than bouncing dots, but the horses followed.

The Phantom rushed away from his family, toward the sound.

Muscular and gleaming, he flowed like liquid silver around sagebrush and rocks. His flint-hard hooves made every step count. He was homing in on the enemy.

Once, the Phantom had been tame. He might have been tolerant of men, if they hadn't penned him, strangled him with ropes, pursued and nearly poisoned him.

Captivity had taught him not to fear men.

Freedom had taught him to hate them.

Should she go after him? Sam tried to think. She might keep the horse from being shot, but if a stray bullet struck her, she'd be no good to him.

Read the Phantom Stallion books!

AVON BOOKS

An Imprint of HarperCollinsPublishers
www.harperchildrens.com